I0687663

# MONTANA COUNTDOWN

## THE MCALLISTER BROTHERS BOOK TWO

### CRICKET ROHMAN

# MONTANA COUNTDOWN

## Cricket Rohman

This is a work of fiction. Names, characters, places, and incidents are the product of the author's imagination or are used fictitiously. Any resemblance to actual persons, living or dead, business establishments, events, or locales is entirely coincidental.

Copyright © 2018 by Cricket Rohman

All rights reserved. No part of this book may be reproduced, scanned, or distributed in any printed or electronic form without the permission of the author.

Cover design & interior formatting by:
Sweet 'N Spicy Designs

Coyote photo by author Shreve Stockton at www.dailycoyote.net

ISBN: 978-0-9994819-7-4
Ebook ISBN: 978-0-9994819-6-7

## Acknowledgments

I would like to say thank you to:

All of my West Dolores friends who spread the word of my books' existence and sent encouragement my way.

My talented and truthful editor, Amir. My story is better because of him.

Jaycee, my formatter/cover designer for her infinite patience and wonderful work.

Author of *The Daily Coyote*, Shreve Stockton. She graciously allowed me to use the photo of her coyote pup, Charlie on Montana Countdown's back cover.

Wild coyotes — the 4-legged kind. Their survival skills inspire and amaze me.

NOVELS BY CRICKET ROHMAN

**Saving Madeline**

*Standalone Contemporary Fiction*

**The McAllister Brothers Series**

*Romantic Western Adventures*

Colorado Takedown

Montana Countdown

Wyoming Sundown

**The Creative Hearts Sweet Romance Series**

*Creative Women Novellas*

Phoebe's Photo Fetish

Anna's Animal House

Caitlin's Cow Wash

Tina's Tasty Tours

**The Lindsey Lark Series**

*Fiction with Elements of Romance & Mystery*

Wanted: An Honest Man

Letters, Lovers, & Lies

Hit The Road, Jake!

**The Fantasy Maker Series**

*Contemporary Adventures*

Forever Island

Winter's Blush

*This book is dedicated to*

*Jerry, Justin*

*and*

*Real Cowboys Everywhere*

# HOT WATER, THE WILD WOMAN, & THE EQUINE BODYGUARD

## ONE

Ivy Radcliff tried not to cry as she sat hidden in a dark corner of the Denver bar, slowly sipping a beer. Listening to the doctor's unexpected words had been tough, even depressing. She reminded herself that life was not always fair. Every day on the job was proof of that, except this time, she was the recipient of such unfairness.

Staring down into her drink, she watched a tear drop into the golden liquid, proving that crying in your beer wasn't an old saying; it was her new reality. Still, she wanted no part of the pitiful sensation overtaking her body. That was not her style.

She took a gulp and gritted her teeth, trying like hell to snap out of it and move forward, but lecturing herself had little effect. Action. She was a woman of action and needed to do something, anything, right now. If a funk saturated with negativity lingered at her feet long enough, she'd sink downward to join it. She'd been there once before and vowed never to return. Could she find happiness knowing what she knows? Saving others came naturally. Saving herself, not so much.

The sound of multiple sirens zooming by outside caught her attention, and her body immediately reacted, flooding her bloodstream with adrenaline. Ivy jerked her head toward the window and jumped to her feet, ready to engage. Her heart pounded, her muscles ready for action, but then she remembered that she was off-duty. She sighed, waved to the waitress for one last beer, and sat back down. Ordering the drink was the only action she'd come up with. For the moment, it beat going home to an empty apartment.

"Here you go, miss." The waitress placed the icy mug on the small table. "Can I get you anything else?"

Food. She should eat something. A salad? Some lean protein? Nope, not tonight. A little grease and a little salt would do the trick. It was time to indulge. She ordered a basket of fries, and when it arrived, she asked the waitress to bring her bill. She'd be leaving soon.

The waitress turned, hesitated, and looked back at Ivy. "You know, hon, in my line of work, I meet a lot of people from all walks of life and in all sorts of moods.

You look like you have a lot on your mind. Are you all right?"

The question came out of left field, startling Ivy. How could this total stranger know she had problems? Were they that apparent? Her poker face needed work. "I'm fine. Everything's fine, thanks." She felt her cheeks rise, forming a fake smile.

"Okay, but I'm here if you need to talk," said the waitress using a motherly tone.

Ivy nodded blankly and began munching the hot, salty fries. She needed to man up and change the subject of her dismal thoughts. After all, it wasn't as if she had a life-threatening disease. But what could she do? What might help?

Recently, she had unburied her life-long dream and proclaimed her desire to write the great American novel. Fortunately, only the walls in her apartment were privy to her declaration. Initially – having never written much of anything – she saw writing as a divine hobby that would fill her off-duty hours. *Who am I kidding? I can't come up with an idea for a story, let alone 75,000 words.* The funk at her feet had risen to her knees. Damn!

With her glass half empty and the fries all gone, she stood to leave. A good night's sleep in that empty apartment now called to her. That's when she overheard a guy sitting at the bar rambling on and on, something about keys and the number seven. A birth date, perhaps? A horse he planned to purchase or bet on? He *was* wearing a cowboy hat. Her keen interest in numerology, plus a story-telling cowboy with a chiseled body talking about numbers, equaled the perfect distraction from her current state of mind.

Ivy casually moved to a closer table and sat back down, hoping to hear the man's words, his story, more clearly, even though the hour was late. The kind waitress came by with a cup of coffee.

"Thought you could use this," she said with a smile. "Just so you know, I'm clocking out, and the bartender is closing up in about twenty minutes."

Ivy nodded and reached for her bag.

"The coffee is on the house. Enjoy. I mean that."

If only she could stay awake and alert for another hour, she'd have enough time to round up more details about the cowboy's keys and numbers, and make it home safely. Digging deep into her bag, she found a pen but no paper. No problem. She'd write her notes on a napkin. Better than nothing. Before she'd written a single word, she felt like a writer for the first time in her life.

Poised and ready to write, she waited, but the cowboy stopped talking. Ivy looked up and saw why. He had no one to talk to. The bartender had taken a drink to the only other person left in the bar – an older man dressed in black sitting with his back to her.

"Last call, ma'am. Need anything else?" Ivy shook her head. Then he asked the cowboy, "How about one more?"

He gave a thumbs-up and continued where he'd left off with his rambling. "A rancher can't be too careful. He's got a lot more to look after than just his cows and horses. That's where I come in." He glanced from side to side as if making certain no one else would hear what he'd say next and lowered his voice to almost a whisper. "There is one ranch in Montana loaded with treasure, enough treasure to make an honest man go rogue, and I know the secret to keeping that fortune safe."

A fortune? Treasure? All on a ranch in Montana? With newfound stamina, sleep became the furthest thing from Ivy's mind. She scribbled the words Montana, treasure, ranch, and secrets on the napkin and kept listening. The only other patron appeared to be listening too.

"Just how does one man keep all that treasure safe?" the guy behind the bar asked.

The cowboy hesitated, drumming his fingers on the bar's surface. Ivy wondered if he'd answer that question.

"What I can tell you is this... without the seven special keys, keeping the rancher's treasure safe would be impossible."

With only ten minutes until closing time and an unexpected pause in the cowboy's story, Ivy made a quick, necessary dash to the Ladies' Room. She'd only been gone a minute, but when she returned, the man in black nearly knocked her down as he hurried from the bar. The storyteller was nowhere to be seen.

Unable to hear every word the cowboy spoke, details of his unique story were missing. She spent the next half hour talking to the bartender as he cleaned and closed up.

"Do you think he was spouting fact or fiction?" To her, however, it didn't matter. She'd made up her mind.

The bartender laughed. "That's a nice way to phrase your question. I hear a lot of stories, and they're mostly lies. I guess you'd call that fiction."

"You think his story was all lies?"

"Most stories are. This guy was different, though. I'm not sure I believed his story, but I believed him. Don't ask me to make sense of that because it doesn't."

He didn't have much more to add except for the name of the Montana ranch the cowboy had mentioned. She'd heard enough to begin formulating a rough premise for a novel, a mystery, one she'd never have thought of on her own. Excited about the new project that had fallen into her lap and the research required to write such a story, she made a hasty, impulsive decision.

She left a phone message for her boss informing him

that beginning tomorrow, she'd be taking her vacation days, which had accumulated over the past few years. He wouldn't be happy, she could even lose her job, but considering the devastating news from earlier that day and her desire to finally write a novel, it was what her gut told her to do. Could she live with the outcome of becoming jobless? Maybe. Change is good, right? Could she live with the current sadness she felt? Definitely not!

Ivy hurried home to plan her trip to The Lonely Horse Ranch if there were such a place.

LAST WEEK, Troy McAllister had a brief and long-overdue visit with his parents. He usually avoided their company, but guilt rose to a level he could not ignore, and that uncomfortable feeling was the motivation he needed to finally make the trip.

Fortunately, they hadn't confronted him about his personal life this time. No nagging him to find a girl, fall in love, and get married, which was part of almost every conversation they had over the past decade. Instead, they discussed the two horses due to give birth in a month and the weather. All in all, a tolerable visit, but he was glad to be back at his Montana ranch. He had no desire to spend his days anywhere else.

Troy loved the lavish lifestyle his horse breeding business provided. The ranch was his personal playground, where he could do what he wanted when he wanted. The cattle, the trail horses, and the cabins were there for the purpose of entertaining the guests who arrived every year to take part in a dude-ranch experience. He'd made wise decisions when hiring his staff. They were more than capable of handling all the guest service aspects of the dude-ranch side of his business while he focused on management, revenue intake, and targeted marketing.

Though he'd never admit it out loud, he also enjoyed the "hot cowboy" reputation invented and circulated by the local horse-riding women. It suited him. He was a good-looking man, and he knew it. The only missing link from his perfect life was *hero status*. He wouldn't admit that out loud either, but he longed to be a hero, to tackle some noteworthy action so the world and his father might take notice. A mere fantasy, of course. Such a golden opportunity was unlikely to show itself on the ranch.

He made his rounds to the main barn, the bunkhouse, the guests' registration lobby, and the kitchen, as he did every morning. Just as he approached The Lodge, his cell phone rang.

"Hi, Mom. Is something wrong?"

"No, dear. Your father and I got to talking and realized we hadn't completed our conversation with you."

"Troy," said Clint, "I've pressed the speaker button so we can all hear each other."

Troy kicked at the dirt. He had work he wanted to do. Could he maintain civility when his personal life was about to be discussed, again? On speakerphone, no less. He cut them off at the pass.

"Mom, Dad, nothing has changed. Got no plans for marriage. No plans for kids. I'm too busy working the ranch."

"Son, I've got no problem with your work ethic, but you're not getting any younger you know. Your little brother has a wonderful woman in his life now. We've never seen him happier."

Troy wished he could please his parents, especially his dad, but that would require a significant change in his lifestyle. He liked his playboy reputation and didn't think he had it in him to settle down and be a family man. That scenario was not in his future.

"Dad, I'm not Trace and—" SMACK! CLATTER! CRACK! The loud noise interrupted his comment. Just as well, they wouldn't have liked what he was about to say. "Got to go."

# TWO

Ivy walked through The Lonely Horse Ranch's lodge noting its shelves filled with leather-bound books, the walls decorated with sepia-toned portraits and wildlife photos, and the lingering smell of wood smoke. A bar, resembling an old-fashioned saloon complete with tall stools and liquor bottles lined up in front of a mirror, covered a good part of the far wall.

Delighted to have this amazing room all to herself for the moment, Ivy's imagination went wild as she pictured it filled with people from days gone by. This lodge was made for action. Or was it merely part of the ranch's décor and only for the purpose of creating an old western atmosphere? Whatever its purpose, it made her feel nostalgic, transporting her back to those rougher, romanticized days.

As she looked around, possible settings and scenarios for her first story overwhelmed her thoughts. A dark hallway at the far end of the great room just beyond the bar caught her eye, but it was the door about twenty feet to the right of the hallway and standing slightly ajar that captured her interest. *I wonder what's behind door number one.*

Overcome with curiosity, she stepped closer for a quick peek. Delighted that her mind kicked into research mode without any prompting, she felt compelled to enter the room.

Ivy thought she might be trespassing, but what harm could come from looking around? The door was unlocked, not even closed all the way, so no one could call it breaking and entering. She'd neither touch nor damage anything. Besides, the thrill of snooping around the ranch for the sake of research for her book kept the doctor's words and her sadness at bay. She proceeded with enthusiastic caution.

Standing in the middle of the dimly lit room, she rotated her body like slow-moving chopper blades and took it all in. The floors were covered with several Navajo rugs and runners. Was this a man cave or simply rugged, western décor? On her second rotation, she caught a glimpse of it – an elegant portrait of a man and a woman, probably the owners of the ranch, hanging on the wall behind a massive, mahogany desk. That's when her capricious imagination kicked in.

After looking over her shoulder and giving her sudden, brilliant idea a two-second thought, she stepped lightly toward the mammoth work of art. She'd seen the movies. She'd read the stories. Her gut told her that something was hidden behind that portrait. She'd take a quick peek, nothing more, and then move on to other areas of the ranch.

Her hand, now on the portrait's bottom corner, began to shift it a mere inch to the left and away from the wall. Before she'd taken a good look, the floor beneath her feet moved as if it were a conveyer belt. How was that even possible? A sudden attack of vertigo? An earthquake? Caught off guard, she screamed as her legs flew out from under her and she fell to the floor. The shock was one thing, the physical pain another. The portrait followed suit with a loud crash as a shadowy figure retreated around the corner.

*Do I have competition? Two writers in search of the same story?*

Face down on the floor, Ivy groaned. Her job back home gave her plenty of experience with pain, other people's pain, but never her own. Raising her head, she focused her eyes on the space previously hidden by the portrait. She was right, there it was. A safe! An unusual safe. It resembled a tiny metal door recessed into the wall. From her prone position, the lock appeared to be a standard deadbolt that anyone with the correct key could open. She'd think of this as key number one and began imagining what treasure the safe might contain.

When Ivy attempted to push herself up from the floor, hot pain shot through her arms, and a wave of nausea followed. She managed to roll onto her side wanting to give her body a few minutes to recuperate before trying again.

Her mind, however, remained active. Unless the ranch was haunted, someone had been in the room with her. Someone instigated her fall. Though slender, she was fit and strong and in excellent health, except for that one issue. No, she would not have fallen without some external cause at work, and that cause had departed quickly.

She pulled her hand-held recorder from her pocket, flicked the record switch, and whispered, "Someone didn't want me to discover that wall safe. All the more reason to—"

SLAM! The sudden sound sent a violent jolt through her body. Her heart raced again. What now? It would be foolish for someone who didn't want to be seen to make a loud noise or slam a door on his or her way out. That made no sense.

She heard the voice before she saw the man.

"Just what the hell do you think you're doing?"

She was caught red-handed, but this was no cookie jar. Sprawled awkwardly on the floor behind the massive mahogany desk, Ivy's wide-open eyes stared at a muddied-up cowboy wearing a black hat. His hands rested on his narrow hips as he glared down at her.

"Sorry, I was just—"

"Snooping around a private office? Follow me out to the main room of The Lodge so I can restate the ranch rules and policies that you seem to have forgotten already." He turned, heading toward the door, then spoke into some type of intercom or walkie-talkie requesting someone from maintenance to come to the office to repair the frame and re-hang the portrait. He listened for a moment, then said, "Yeah, a misplaced guest. I'll tell you about it later."

Ivy stood and plodded behind him, one foot then the other, like a child headed for the principal's office. In a matter of seconds, she needed to come up with a legiti-mate-sounding reason, a story, even a lie if necessary, for her presence in that room.

Thoughts dashed through her mind. For a twenty-nine-year-old woman who'd dreamed of becoming a novelist and until now had never taken any action to make her dream come true, she'd convinced herself that booking two weeks at *this* ranch was a good first step. She'd begin by writing a fictional short story; that should be easy. After all, she'd been given an idea that night in the bar. An idea that fit neatly with her interest in numerology. She'd expand that story later, turning it into a novel. But first things first.

"I'm sorry about the portrait," she said, placing one hand behind her back and crossing her fingers. "And I didn't realize the room was so... off limits."

The cowboy turned and pointed to the sign above the door where the words *Private Office* were clearly printed.

Feeling guilty and defensive, she blurted out, "I don't see the words *No Trespassing* or *Do Not Enter*."

"Of course you don't. That would be rude." The cowboy's stern demeanor should have convinced her to walk away, or at least stop talking, but it didn't.

"Why don't they just keep the room locked if its contents are so valuable? Then you wouldn't risk such a scene as this one."

"What's that supposed to mean?" The cowboy frowned and adjusted his hat.

"For starters, yelling at one of the ranch's paying guests can't be good for business, and doesn't this establishment follow the well-known saying *the customer is always right?*" Ivy knew she was the person in the wrong. Still, she kept on talking. "I bet your boss would much prefer that policy. I know I would."

The guy grinned. Or was it a smirk? Either way, now that the conversation appeared to be over, she noticed a few details beyond the cowboy's cold manner and his black hat. Wisps of sandy brown hair poking below his hat, open snaps on his western shirt exposing the top third of his chest, tight-fitting jeans, and dusty boots all added to her curiosity. Was he a real cowboy or a fake one? Did it even matter?

For several years she'd been too busy to notice any good-looking men, though they'd likely been around. What was it about this one? She'd seen a few cowboys before and never given them the time of day, let alone a second glance. She backed away, determined to avoid being caught foolishly gawking, which in her mind was far more shameful than snooping.

---

TROY SHOOK HIS HEAD. He'd over-reacted. This feisty woman was correct about a couple of things. She was, after all, a guest at the ranch. And maybe the door should be locked. He'd give that some thought. Hoping for a truce, he reached out and offered his hand. She didn't move. Her hesitation baffled him. He was accustomed to women of all ages taking full vantage of any excuse to be near him.

He put on his best *aw-shucks* smile and stepped closer to her to try again. This time, she reached out and the handshake took place. Troy noticed blood oozing slowly from her forearm and her neck. He'd make sure she received medical attention. But, for the moment, he'd become the hesitator due to an unforeseen distraction. Sparks flickered faintly through his palm and up his arm as his hand grasped hers. What was that all about? Did she feel it too? Troy was not a man fazed by flickers. That word was not even in his vocabulary – until today.

"You've got some bleeding going on there," he said, pointing at her arm and touching her neck. "I think you should stop by the first aid office. It's on the south side of the ranch hands' bunkhouse. You'll see a red **X** on the door." Watching her walk away, he wondered what made her so damn interesting. "Hey, you're headed in the wrong direction. Want an escort?"

"No thanks. I can take care of this with soap and water and a small bandage. Don't need your help."

Her comment stung like a slap in the face. He didn't know how to handle rejection coming from a woman. It had never happened before.

# THREE

Troy rarely ate in the guests' dining room. He preferred to grab a bite with the men at the chuck wagon or fix his own meals in the ranch kitchen after the guests had been fed. When he entertained a woman, his personal residence was the cooking and dining location of choice. Preparing a home-cooked, gourmet meal faired far better than dinner and a movie in town. Besides, that would be too much like a date. He enjoyed the no-commitment flings he engaged in now and then, but he enjoyed his freedom more. Today, however, he'd dine with his guests. Ulterior motive? Sure thing.

"Is this seat taken?" He sat down before she had time to respond.

Ivy shrugged, chewed, and swallowed. "I don't think

so unless you allow invisible ghosts to sit here." She passed Troy the bowl of potato salad. The meals were always served family style.

"What brings you to The Lonely Horse Ranch?" Most of the guests were couples or families. A woman flying solo was rare, so he was curious.

"Fresh air, relaxation, and I might write a bit." She paused in thoughtful contemplation. "And I desperately needed a break from my day job."

Kitchi, Troy's right-hand man and food service manager, stopped by their table. "Good to see you in the dining hall, Mr. McAllister. I see you've met Miss Ivy." The Native American man raised his all-knowing brows. "Enjoy your meals," said Kitchi, and with a grin on his face, he walked away.

Good to know her name, but what was going on with Kitchi? That brief encounter was completely out of character for him.

Between the main course and dessert, Ivy asked, "Do you have any family here at the ranch?"

He gave a negative headshake and helped himself to a serving of peach cobbler.

Ivy persisted with her questions. "Do you have family anywhere?"

Not willing to share personal information, he came up with a suitable, though vague answer. "I have a mother, a father, and a younger brother." He thought he detected a slight flinch and quick wave of sadness on her beautiful face. Yes, she was beautiful in a natural way. No doubt about that.

Lunch over, he walked her down the hallway and out through The Lodge. His curiosity not yet satisfied, he offered to give her a tour of the entire ranch tomorrow morning at ten, hoping to discover what made this spunky woman tick.

"You brought a pair of jeans, right?" he asked, and after she nodded he continued, "Good. Let's meet here at my office tomorrow." He pointed to the *Private Office* sign for the second time today.

"That's your office? What is your job here?"

He glanced around the immediate area. Why was he stalling? Typically, he couldn't wait to boast about his connection to the ranch. "I guess I do a little bit of everything." It had not occurred to him that she was unaware that the ranch, The Lodge, the cabins, the horses, and everything as far as the eye could see belonged to him. But then she'd just arrived late yesterday and probably hadn't had the opportunity to visit the grounds or read any of the books and magazines that explained the history of the place. She didn't ask any more questions, so he didn't elaborate.

"See you tomorrow. I'll be easy to spot because I'll be

the girl wearing jeans." She gave him a teasing smile and walked away.

Troy frowned. Ivy spoke to him in a tone he was not accustomed to. It wasn't the slightest bit seductive – the tone he was most familiar with – instead, it had a playful edge to it. Did he like that? He'd have fun finding out.

---

EVER SINCE IVY'S ARRIVAL, she'd experienced a bizarre sensation of being watched. The feeling grew stronger earlier that morning when she walked from her cabin to the dining hall, and then again when she snooped around in Troy's private office. Yes, she'd been snooping, but these creepy feelings were ridiculous. Get a grip. Shake it off. *I'm not the nervous, paranoid type.*

After a brief rest at her cabin, she returned to The Lodge and plopped down in a comfy leather chair facing Troy's office. She involved herself with people watching while taking a few notes in the name of research. She also jotted down everything she could remember about that morning's mishap including the unexplainable moving rug, the broken portrait, as well as herself behaving badly, thinking one or more of these gems would end up in one of her stories someday.

Looking up from her notepad as she contemplated

how to transform her wandering words into a scene, Ivy caught a glimpse of... what? A shadow? A reflection darting around the corner? She ruled out the guests since there were none left in the large room, but who or what could it be? Perhaps that moving, elusive object would reappear if she were not visible. However, if she left, she might never know who had orchestrated her fall, but if she stayed, would she be the victim of another injury?

*Putting myself in danger for the sake of a story? Not wise.* But she felt that was exactly what an adventurous author would do.

Curiosity conquered caution. Ivy hid behind the huge leather chair and sat on the floor in a cross-legged position. She waited, trying to be still and patient having no desire to engage in any type of confrontation. For the moment, all she wanted was to identify the lurking *thing* and learn why it was here at the ranch following her around.

But what if it was confrontational? Feeling her heart beat rapidly and noticing the dampness of her palms, she quickly switched to a crouched position that would allow her to spring into action if necessary.

Still waiting, a variety of creative speculations crossed her mind, though she wrote none of them down. *What if a dangerous, dominating figure – holding a gun – entered the room or a haunting apparition glided by? It is*

*October.* Her thoughts stopped, interrupted by the sound of a creaking floorboard. *There goes the ghost theory.* Had her patience finally paid off?

Hearing the creaking sound again, she peeked around the side of the chair. Something moved, but so fast and fleeting that it disappeared before she got a good look. Had she been spotted? Shrugging, she got up and made herself comfortable in the large leather chair, then struggled to form a picture in her mind's eye from a mere glimpse at the unknown. It seemed to have a human shape, or was it more like the branch of a tree? Either way, it was skinny. A man? Maybe. A woman? Or an optical illusion? A definitive answer eluded her.

One thing was certain. She'd seen something and smelled a whiff of smoke, and she doubted ghosts or shadows smoked. This person, this thing, would remain an *it* until she had some answers and a better look. She hadn't seen any anorexic-like humans in the dining room or anywhere on the grounds, so she remained steadfast in her assumption that no ranch guests were involved. But then who?

If this shadow, this entity, was responsible for her fall earlier today, another fact came to mind. *It* was capable of pulling rugs out from under a person like a magician whisking a tablecloth from a flat surface, except that this magician's dishes – that would be Ivy – crashed to the floor. *Was it on purpose to get her away from the safe? Or just to make noise so she'd be discovered?*

Unafraid, because no serious harm had come to her, curiosity tickled her thinking again. Perhaps this phenomenon and the existence of *it* would ensure the presence of an antagonist in her story and enhance the plot, or was that the conflict, or the story question? She didn't know, being so new to writing, but it felt like it would be essential to the plot. *I've got a lot to learn.*

Her mind began to wander. Thoughts of a stalker came fast and furiously. But no one back in Denver knew the location of her get-away. No one had a reason to follow her here. Why would they? Her personal life was mundane, almost non-existent. No way would she be of interest to a stalker. Didn't they go after hookers? The only hooking she'd ever done involved a fish. She wanted this mini-mystery solved. Or did she? A twinge of excitement flowed through her like the liquid in a can of Red Bull.

Then, so typical of Ivy, semi-logical thinking took over. This Creeping Stick – her new and improved name for *it* because *IT* was already taken by another author – might be the owner's private bodyguard. No, that was not the word she was looking for. *I need my thesaurus.* But within a few seconds, the desired term popped up in her head. Of course, an in-house security guy. That would make more sense. There seemed to be a lot of assets to protect here right out in the open, not to mention hidden treasure. But unless the Creeping Stick was good with a gun, it would be incapable of keeping anything secure. How tough could a stick be? She laughed. Was her mystery morphing into a goofy comedy? Perhaps. Either way, she was having the time of her life.

Still, Ivy vowed to trust her intuition, her senses, and pay greater attention to any hair-raising feelings, even in the absence of visual proof. To solidify her conviction, she'd keep her small, hand-held recorder close-by at all times and capture any thoughts, real or imagined. All of which would come in handy as she began to outline her story. Just today, several important ideas were lost forever because she hadn't had the time to write them down, and she'd left the recorder in the cabin. She'd never make that mistake again.

Smiling, she headed toward the front door, pleased that not one tear had fallen from her eyes during her brief time at the ranch. But then, without her permission, her thoughts made a sudden and unpleasant U-turn. No tears, but maybe fears.

*What if the Creeping Stick is a stalker who selected me at random just because I'm here? No, that's a TV thing, not a ranch thing. But still...*

# FOUR

Troy didn't know Ivy's last name, but he knew where to find it. The gravel on the path crunched beneath his boots as he headed over to the registration desk in the lobby of the guest services building.

"Saige?" No response came. Where was she? She wouldn't leave her post when airport shuttles filled with new guests were expected throughout the day. He'd looked forward to a conversation with her. "Saige?" he called again and stepped behind the counter. Except for one slightly crooked painting, everything appeared to be in order, so she hadn't left while in the middle of a transaction. Probably just a ladies' room break.

He wandered into the back office with the intention of finding Ivy's check-in paperwork from yesterday but was derailed from his mission. He stared blankly at the walls, his mouth slightly agape.

Every piece of western art and each framed photo was in disarray as if a tornado had passed through. Saige knew he was a stickler about symmetry, order, and having everything in its place, so she would not have left the pictures like that. On the other hand, there'd been no storm, no wind at all, no obvious reason for what he was witnessing. Any logical explanation for the disarray of the office artwork eluded his thinking.

Troy, known for his quick thinking, was suddenly struck by a vision of Ivy, the pretty guest he'd found sprawled on the floor of his office near the fallen family portrait. He was also known for his rare, but quick temper. And now he wondered if she was involved in any of the recent vandalism. Was she up to something?

Then he laughed at the thought of her having an art and photo fetish. Nope, that was too crazy. It wasn't a big deal, but where was Saige, and who messed with the art on these walls? Why would anyone do that?

The bells attached to the entrance jingled. Good, she was back. Troy went to greet her and make sure everything was all right. She must know something about the crooked artwork. A logical reason would ease his mind. Stopping in his tracks, his jaw dropped. He'd come face to face with Ivy, who appeared as surprised as he was.

"Hi." They spoke the small greeting in unison.

"Ah, the girl wearing jeans. How's your arm?" He smiled, turning on the well-practiced charm he reserved for pretty women.

A twinkle formed in her eyes. "Fine." She reached up and gave his deltoid a playful punch. "How's yours?"

"Never been better. Have you got a minute? I want to ask you something."

"Got more than a minute. I've got almost two weeks. So, ask away."

Not wanting to admit that he'd been in search of her surname, he reached out his hand as if to shake it.

"Wow! A little déjà vu going on here. What's up, cowboy?"

Damn, she was one spunky gal. He added an extra dose of charm to his reply. "Since I'm here, and there you are, it seemed like a good time for a proper introduction. My name is Troy McAllister. What's yours, ma'am?"

Tilting her head, she reached out her hand. "Ivy. Ivy Radcliff. Pleased to meet you, Mr. McAllister."

Troy tapped his cowboy-booted foot and adjusted his hat before asking his remaining questions. "I wanted to speak with Saige, the registrar. Have you seen her?"

"Sure. I met her when I checked in. Haven't seen her today though."

He stepped over to one of the crooked paintings on

the wall by the entrance and straightened it, then turned to watch her reaction. Seeing no change in her expression, he said, "Follow me. I want to show you something." He led her into the back office where he pointed out the numerous pieces of oddly hanging framed photos and art. "Since you appeared at the scene of the previous wall-hanging crime, thought you might shed some light on this one."

"Nope," Ivy responded with a shrug. "No light. Not even a glimmer."

Unable to tolerate or ignore the disarray, Troy began to straighten the artwork. Ivy jumped right in to help. Every time she straightened a painting or a photo, she stood back and seemed to study it, or was she admiring her own picture-hanging ability?

"How did you acquire so much interesting, old-time cowboy art?"

"Been collecting art and artifacts for about fifteen years. I'm not much for going shopping, so I found a lot of it on the Internet. Occasionally, I'll pick something up at an art auction."

Troy kept a watchful eye for Saige, expecting she'd return before they'd completed the art-straightening task. When she didn't, he started to worry. Her absence was odd. He'd handpicked each and every member of The Lonely Horse Ranch staff and knew they were dependable, hardworking, and loyal. For Saige to leave the front desk unmanned, something unusual must have taken place. He wanted to pace or at least look for her, but instead, he escorted Ivy out to the front porch, stalling, waiting on a woman. He sat down on the glider and patted the space next to him. "What does a pretty lady like you do with her time when she's not vacationing at a Montana dude ranch?"

Ivy accepted his invitation and sat beside him. "Oh, I'm not really vacationing. I wanted to be somewhere peaceful that would provide me with some uninterrupted writing time. I'm a – she paused, thinking, then flaunted a mischievous smile – a travel writer. If you must know, I'm working on a few demo pieces to use when applying for part-time writing assignments. This place is perfect for that."

Troy reached behind her, resting his arm on the back of the glider. "How's that coming along?"

"I do have a good feeling about this location," she said, her eyes drifting to some far away place. "I've walked around the main buildings, exploring here and there, thinking about words that describe what I see."

Troy knew women, and something was off about her delivery. He wasn't buying her travel-writer story. "You do know the rules of your trade, right? You can't publish anything you write about the ranch without the owners permission."

"Of course." Unfazed, using her feet, Ivy set the glider in motion and they rocked gently. "How do you fill your spare time? What do you do when you're not working at the ranch?"

The way she changed the subject from her to him so quickly led him to believe she was lying or, at least, stretching the truth. Why would she do that? He didn't care what she did with her time. "I'm always at the ranch doing jobs I love to do, so I don't think of it as work. Several times a year I visit my parents."

Now Troy was the one to pause. His words prompted a guilty feeling since he'd only visited once during the past eighteen months. "I spend my time riding horses, herding cattle, and gearing up for the opening of the ranch's newest service – taking tourists, photographers, and hunters on overnight backcountry adventures. We hope to have that operational by spring."

"Your parents live in Denver?"

He was caught off guard by her question, positive he hadn't mentioned where they lived. "As a matter of fact, they live just outside of Denver. Ever been there?"

Ivy's foot began to tap the air. "Sure. Hasn't everybody?"

The approaching sound of many horses cantering and

whinnying put their conversation on hold. The weekly riding group of young women had arrived and, as was their custom, they rode around searching for Troy before entering the arena where they'd rehearse their horseback routines. They were undeniably hot looking women wearing lots of makeup, tight jeans, and sleeveless t-shirts with plenty of sequins.

Spotting Troy on the porch, they reined in their horses, every woman waving and smiling with bright red lips and white sparkling teeth. *Ah. Just a regular day at The Lonely Horse Ranch.*

"Hi, Troy!" Why did they always speak with sexy, southern drawls? Most of them were born and raised in Montana or they had moved out from the east coast. "We're gonna work on some new choreography with the horses, want to watch?"

He actually did enjoy observing when they practiced their horseback riding routines. It resembled synchronized swimming on dry land, and while the horses were amazing, these talented women displayed more jiggle than most men could endure, especially his wranglers.

"Some other time, ladies. Got work to do. Enjoy your day," he said, tipping his hat. Moans and groans filled the air, and pouting red lips begged him to change his mind before they galloped off to the arena.

Troy took Ivy's hand. "I know it's not ten o'clock yet,

but since we're both right here, what do you say we begin our tour of the property?" That way he could keep an eye out for Saige too.

"Thought you had work to do?" A playful smile formed on her pretty face.

"I am working. I'm taking you on a tour of the ranch." Disappointed in his lackluster response, he added, "And I anticipate that will be a challenge."

They walked and talked, and their good-natured bantering continued. But something nagged at him, though he couldn't put a finger on it.

"I'd like to make this a threesome. Any objections?"

She stopped, looking up with amused eyes. "You're the tour guide. The more the merrier."

Troy led the way to the stables. First, he showed her the tack room and the large whiteboard on the wall that listed the week's riding schedule, feed quantities, and medication or supplement needs. Before he'd finished explaining the organizational system, a horse appeared in the doorway neighing and stomping one of its front hooves. Troy patted the horse on the neck, grabbed a lead rope from a hook on the wall, and attached it to the horse's halter.

"Ivy, I'd like you to meet Tracker, my main horse. Tracker, this is Ivy." The horse neighed and snorted loudly in response and joined them as the tour continued. "I spend as much time with him as I can."

The next phase of Troy's tour consisted of all the areas occupied by the trail horses, their stalls, corrals, hitching posts and, lastly, the barn.

As the threesome emerged from the barn, Saige hurried toward them, brushing the hair from her forehead and catching her breath. "Oh, there you are. I've been looking all over for you, Troy."

Troy scratched his head and handed Ivy Tracker's lead rope before pulling Saige aside. "And why were you doing that?"

"Because I got an urgent call saying that you needed to see my right way."

"Who called?"

She shifted her weight from leg to leg, eyes squinting. "Actually, I'm not sure. The man spoke so fast, and the connection was bad. And then the line went dead. I thought something terrible had happened and—"

"Slow down, Saige. Everything is fine, and the mystery is solved. Well, at least one of them is." Troy motioned for Ivy to come closer allowing her to hear the conversation. He'd watch her reaction wondering if she'd have anything to add or cover up.

"Mysteries? More than one?" Saige, an avid mystery reader, begged for the details.

Details? Their numbers were few. Troy explained that he was puzzled when Saige was not at the front desk or in her office when he stopped by. At least now he knew why she wasn't there, though the details were still sketchy.

"I'd better get back. I've been gone almost twenty minutes already." She turned and walked rapidly away.

"Saige," Troy called. "How did all the wall art look before you left your office?"

She stopped and shrugged, a puzzled look on her face. "Fine. Just fine."

"Okay. Thanks." Troy took up Ivy's hand again but quickly let it go. Why was he holding this woman's hand? He wasn't the handholding type, and she certainly didn't need any assistance walking around the ranch. Or did she? He continued the tour, though his heart wasn't in it now. Mystery number two – the assault on the artwork in Saige's office – the mystery he'd not shared with her, gave him a lot more to think about. Silence reigned.

Ivy filled the quiet space. "It seems there's quite a bit going on here. The ranch must have a large staff."

He nodded affirmatively. "Wranglers and housekeepers, stuff like that."

She added to his short list. "I suppose the ranch must also employ food service assistants, security, general maintenance, a medic, a personal bodyguard, carpen—"

He laughed and out of the blue began to speak with an

exaggerated Texas accent. "Whoa, there. Hold your horses, ma'am. Personal bodyguard? Why in the world would you suggest that? Do ya think I need one?"

Ivy stood still and appeared to give his question some serious thought. "Well... you can probably handle the wayward art culprit, but from the looks of the ladies' riding group, yes, I think you do need a bodyguard."

# FIVE

With the midday meal over, the guests scattered – some took a trail ride, others hiked, and a small group did nothing at all – Ivy took out her recorder and took verbal notes about her morning, the main focus being the odd phone call to Saige instructing her to find Troy, and the disturbed art. She wondered what Troy was thinking about. He'd said very little after the conversation with Saige.

The puzzling events she'd witnessed during her short time at the ranch were more than enough to warrant a promotion. From that moment on, her simple snooping days were over. Some serious sleuthing pursuits were called for, and she'd begin in the kitchen.

She was relieved to find the guests gone and the

dining area empty. Today's bold research required privacy. The food prep area was quiet except for the hum and swishing sound coming from the dishwasher. She took the liberty of opening a few drawers and pantry doors. Just getting the lay of the land, so to speak. Awestruck by the appearance and impeccable arrangement of the impressive kitchen, Ivy felt an uncharacteristic urge to cook something, but that rare feeling vanished in seconds. The kitchen in her Denver apartment and the cooking-eating area at work never inspired any culinary ventures, and she definitely lacked talent in that area.

"Can I be of service, Miss Ivy?"

Startled by the sudden sound of a man's voice in this quiet space, she turned to see Kitchi carrying a stack of plastic crates. She should have known who it was immediately since he was the only person to call her Miss Ivy.

"I'm impressed with your kitchen." She wasn't using flattery to distract from her presence there. She meant every word.

"The facility is more than adequate."

His straightforward delivery instigated a giggle, which she promptly suppressed. "I thought you, of all people, would call this area a kitchen."

"Why is that?"

"Your name, Kitchi, it's a nickname because you work here in the kitchen, right?"

"No," he said, and almost smiled. "That is my name. It's an Algonquin name. It means brave."

Feeling foolish and wondering if an apology was an appropriate course of action, she searched for her next comment. "Kitchi is a great name. A cool coincidence too."

The man went about his work silently – packing the crates with food, tons of food – as if she wasn't there. Maybe she had said something wrong. Could he be upset by her presence in his territory? Wisely, she saved her burning question about the patch over his eye for later. Now was not the time, but the silence needed to be broken.

"Where are you taking all that food?"

"To the picnic area."

"Let me help. I really want to," she said, and took a step closer, allowing her care giving and helper instincts to kick in. Was that due to the patch covering his eye or the fact that they were about the same size? Ivy was 5'7", which was an ample height for a woman, but small for a man.

She watched him move swiftly around the kitchen as if he'd designed it. He knew the location of every food item and culinary tool without a thought or hesitation, in fact, she was certain he could do it all with his eyes closed. She'd bet money on that. Every time he lifted one of the fully packed crates, the muscles on his slender arms bulged like a bodybuilder flexing for points.

She packed the lighter items: buns, napkins, and marshmallows, then carried those crates to the truck. She enjoyed helping him, though it was obvious now, he didn't need it. He was every bit as strong as any of the men she knew at work. Unable to resist, she asked a question as they unpacked the picnic supplies.

"Hey, Kitchi, I'm curious about the large barn. It's so big. There must be lots of animals or hay or equipment in there, but I've never seen anyone go in or out." Ivy didn't mention the fact that each time she'd attempted to enter the barn, all the doors were locked. She waited for his comment.

Never looking up from his work, Kitchi said, "Not my department."

As they prepared the cookout area for the picnic, several wranglers came by and began setting up the grills that would later be lit for cooking that night's cowboy dinner. A variety of rustic-looking tables and chairs were delivered via a flatbed truck, even a port-a-potty disguised as a rustic outhouse was brought in and strategically placed out of view. The scurry of activity was mind-boggling.

"This isn't just any old picnic, is it?"

"No, it's the famous McAllister Friday Night Cookout and Bonfire. You will like it."

Ivy wrinkled her nose and shook her head. "I don't know. I'm not much into group activities unless I'm the one in charge."

Kitchi's one eye looked into hers with unwavering intensity. "You must come. Everyone attends."

---

TYPICALLY, mingling with the ranch guests was not high on Troy's list, but tonight was an exception. He loved Friday nights, his night of the week to shine and feel important, likely the closest he'd ever get to being a hero.

According to the surveys, the guests loved this weekly event too, always giving the cookout a five-star rating. He expected a large group. All the guest rooms and cabins were occupied, and if tonight were like all the other Friday nights, everyone would show up. That's what Troy hoped for.

He appreciated the employees that stuck around to help out, even though they had already put in a full day's work. Every Friday night during the height of the tourist season, they showed up with smiling enthusiasm. Three wranglers assisted Kitchi with the cooking and serving.

Later, they'd keep the bonfire roaring. Saige poured drinks: beer, wine, soda, and cowboy coffee, and as long as she was referred to as the mixologist, she was happy. She'd also point folks in the direction of the outhouse, if necessary.

No one seemed to mind the extra hours, and though Kitchi, Saige, and the wranglers said on more than one occasion that they'd work the cookouts for free, Troy paid them well.

Troy visited with the guests, shaking hands, giving and receiving hugs, talking up a storm, as well as listening. He made it his mission to bring a smile to every guest's face. Now and then, he managed to take a bite of a burger.

Tonight, however, would be different. His eyes scanned the area watching for Ivy. He wanted her to be there to enjoy the event, the food, and the fun, but he also wanted to impress her. He argued with himself over that thought. He didn't need to impress any woman, not even her.

"Hey, good looking."

Troy turned around and there she stood, her hands on her hips. "That's my line, lady." He wrapped his arms around her and whispered in her ear. "You made it. I'm glad."

Ivy stepped back, her eyes sparkling in the light of the lanterns. "Good observation. I'm here. Here in the flesh!"

"Yes, ma'am, I can see that." Literally, he could see more of her skin tonight than ever before. Though she wore a jean jacket, she'd left it unbuttoned exposing a silky, white, low-cut top that left little to his imagination. Troy escorted her to the campstools that circled the fire. "Have a seat and warm up while I get you a plate. I can see the cool evening air has chilled you."

Ivy seemed oblivious to his teasing comment, saying, "Thanks, I'm fine." Then stood up ready to follow him.

He put his palm up like a traffic cop. "I can take cuts in the line and get the job done in record time. Besides, you don't want to lose your VIP seating, and I don't want you to miss a single minute of the show."

"The show?"

"Yep. Willy, over there, will lead a few sing-a-long songs, someone will tell a few stories, and the marshmallows will roast. Stay put. I'll be back."

By now the line was short. He'd known it would be. He ambled toward the food line, needing information from his right-hand man, Kitchi. "I need a plate for Ivy. Is everybody here?"

"Why do you ask?"

"Because I want to know."

"I see Miss Ivy finally showed up." Kitchi made a sound that resembled a chuckle. He was a serious man, part Algonquin, part mind reader, and he knew Troy better than Troy knew himself. "You are only missing three."

Troy had hoped all the guests would attend. He had a plan, a method to this madness. Tonight, he'd solve a mystery. If the ranch's art vandal sat around this campfire, he'd know. Watching Ivy's expression was part of that plan.

Back at her side, he handed over a blue metal plate piled high with a steak burger, baked beans in a small bowl, and corn on the cob dripping with butter. "Here's a red solo cup filled with cold beer. I can get you something else if you don't want it."

"No, beer's fine. Sit by me."

"I will, later. For now, I'm going to sit directly across from you." He pointed to a vacant seat, then winked. "So I can enjoy the view of your pretty face and your eyes, sparkling in the light of the campfire." Giving compliments was second nature to him. He said things like that to all the women he encountered. He assumed, by Ivy's surprised expression, that she wasn't used to such flattering words... or did she doubt his sincerity?

Head wrangler, Cody, strummed his guitar, and Willy began to sing *She'll Be Comin' Round the Mountain*. Guests joined in as they all found places to sit around the fire, clapping, snapping, and stomping their feet to the rhythm of the music. The wranglers took requests and were able to strum and sing most of them. One teenage boy requested *Who Let the Dogs Out?* Whether they knew that one or not was hard to say. However, the song was neither strummed nor sung.

"You got a story for us tonight, Troy?" Cody asked, as he did every Friday night.

The question was planned. He always had a story, although tonight's was a brand new one. This one had a purpose that required a hasty bit of research. There'd been no time to practice, but he was good at winging it. And so Troy, the storyteller, began.

"This is the story of Rosemary from Salem." He looked intently into each and every pair of eyes gathered around the fire. "Once upon a time, there was a tiny, old woman who lived in a tiny house deep in the woods. Neighbors were few and far between. Her favorite color was blue, and she loved to paint. She painted the walls, and she painted pictures too. What color paint do you think she used?" He paused, but strolled slowly around the fire, again gazing into the guests' eyes. "Well, what do you think?" He put his hand up to his ear as if listening.

"Blue," most called out.

"Right! She hung those blue paintings at eye level,

which for her was only two feet up from the floor. I told you she was tiny. One day, she rode her mini horse far into the woods – I don't know why – and she didn't return until sundown."

A coyote howled from a distant location adding to the ambiance and bringing a smile to Troy's face. Its timing could not have been better.

Troy summoned his most convincing scary voice. He loved the drama, the spinning of yarns, especially when a ghost was involved. The fact that there was a purpose behind this telling magnified his talent. If the art vandal were in the audience, surely he'd flinch, stare at the ground, sneak away, or show some other sign of guilt. Or maybe the vandal was a she. He hadn't ruled out Ivy, though he hoped it wasn't her.

"When the tiny woman returned – even before opening the door of her little house – she felt a mysterious sensation deep down in her tiny bones. Then she entered... and she screamed!"

A scream came from the audience too. Probably Saige. She loved a scary story and was known for adding sound effects to the cookout tales on occasion. Though, this being a new story, even Troy was surprised.

He continued. "Every one of her paintings had been tampered with. On the wall, each painting hung upside down three feet above her tiny head and very far from her eye level." Troy paused, dramatically. Observing his guests all the while. "She cried for the remainder of her life. On quiet nights, people say they can still hear her sobs. Now I ask, who would do such a thing?"

Troy circled the campfire one last time. He stopped and pointed at one of the guests "You?" Then moved to another. "How about you?" He did this a few more times, then took a dramatic bow. "Must have been a ghost," he concluded with a shrug. The guests laughed, cheered, and clapped, but Troy still lacked a suspect.

Families with young kids departed the festivities soon after having their fill of marshmallows and s'mores. Couples, young and not-so-young, began dancing when the sound of modern country pulsed through the crisp night air.

Troy found Ivy helping Kitchi with the cleaning and packing up. "Guests are not allowed to work here," he said, taking her hand and escorting her closer to the campfire. "And, I've saved the last dance for you."

The last dance of the evening was always a slow dance. If a pretty young woman were in the audience without a partner, he'd ask her to dance. If not, he'd look for the sweetest old woman and select her. He knew hours ago that Ivy would be his choice tonight.

Wrapped in his arms, swaying to the music, Ivy

looked up into his eyes. "How'd your secret plan work out?"

He feigned surprise. "What are you talking about?" He prepared for a deltoid punch, which seemed to be her trademark when she felt like teasing, but instead, using both hands she playfully pushed him away.

With hands on her hips, she continued to speak. "At first, I didn't catch on, but when the tiny woman's paintings were moved, your motive was perfectly clear. So, did anyone look away, look nervous—"

His finger on her lips silenced her words. "Shh." He pulled her close to him again, and they swayed to the music. His lips brushed against her ear and he whispered, "Let's enjoy the night, the music, each other." He thought he felt her sweet sigh vibrate gently against his chest. Looking directly into her eyes, it was his turn to sigh. "Your delicious scent, your sparkling eyes – I like everything about you."

Several long seconds passed before she responded to his sweet-talking words. "I'll bet you say that to all the women you slow dance with."

"Okay, you got me there. But this time... I think I mean it."

The music no longer played. Kitchi drove the truck away and the wranglers mounted their horses and headed toward the barn. All alone, Troy and Ivy danced a little longer to the popping sounds of the dying fire, the hoot of an owl, and the distant call of a lone coyote.

"Come on. I'll escort you back to your cabin." He held her hand as they walked by the light of the moon. This had been one of the best McAllister cookouts, maybe THE best, though second thoughts nagged at him about the words he'd spoken to Ivy.

# SIX

Troy stood on the doorstep holding out the palm of his hand. "This is where I ask you for your key so I can unlock and open the door for you. I assume you locked the door."

"Uh, I might have. But, Mr. Ranch Manager, don't you have a master key in one of your pockets? Or maybe a bunch of keys?"

Caught off guard by her question, he merely turned the doorknob and pushed the door open. "Guess you didn't lock it. No need for a key after all."

"Yeah, well, maybe I forgot to lock the door, but I know I left a light on," Ivy said with a frown. "I'm positive about that." The room was pitch black. There wasn't a glimmer of light visible anywhere.

"Stay here. I'll take a look around," said Troy. He

entered the unlocked cabin, flipping the closest light switch. Nothing happened. He tried it a few more times without success and made a mental note to ask maintenance to install new bulbs.

Moving slowly in the darkness, he crossed the main room to give the bathroom light a try. It worked! His sense of relief, however, was cut short by the sound of Ivy's muffled scream. Spinning around, he saw the reason. Someone had been in her cabin. Items from the drawers were strewn across the bed, her purse emptied, and the closet's contents scattered on the floor.

Seeing the stunned expression on her face, he hurried to her side and held her in his arms until she stopped shaking. "I'm so sorry, Ivy. Nothing like this has ever happened here before. Who would do such a thing?" It was a rhetorical question. He hadn't expected a reply.

"I don't know. Maybe it was your art vandal."

She'd made a good point. He wondered if either – or maybe both – of the guests who had not shown up for the cookout could be the culprits of this and the other senseless vandalism. He doubted Ivy had brought any art to the ranch, so why vandalize her cabin? As he stood there holding her, an additional, unwanted idea wormed its way into his thoughts. Could she have staged this mess before coming to the cookout? She did arrive later than the others. How well did he really know her?

He didn't want that scenario to be true and dismissed the idea after recalling her expression and the way she trembled after seeing the condition of her belongings. "I'll get to the bottom of this. That's a promise. Got to make some calls now. I'll be right outside. Are you good with that?"

She nodded and moved away from him as he let go. Taking care not to step on anything, Ivy silently began to sift through the items on the bed and the floor.

Troy, not wanting the news of tonight's problem in a guest's cabin to circulate around the ranch, he called the two most trustworthy people he knew. Kitchi and Saige. He wanted this mess cleaned up quickly, and he'd find a way to make this right for Ivy. On the bright side, he could remove her from his secret list of suspects.

"It's gone. My recorder is gone!" she said, her tone frantic.

"Keep looking. It's got to be in here somewhere. If not, I'll get you another one."

His offer didn't lessen her distress. "You don't understand. All of my latest, greatest thoughts, the ones I'd yet to transcribe, are on that recorder. It's the main tool I use for keeping track of my story ideas and things I observe."

"Story ideas? For travel writing?"

Glancing at the ceiling, she said, "I meant descriptions."

Troy shook his head, not comprehending the level of her distress. "Why would anyone want your recorder?"

Looking directly into his eyes, she sighed deeply. "I have no idea. They're just personal thoughts and unimportant ramblings... only useful to me."

Saige was the first to arrive. After a quick glance at the state of the room, and a wide-eyed, what-the-heck-just-happened look toward Troy, she gave Ivy a hug and began to straighten up the closet. Kitchi arrived and stood frowning in the doorway a few minutes later.

"You okay, Miss Ivy?"

She nodded, convincing no one.

Troy motioned for Kitchi to follow him outside. "Other than our wall-hanging vandalism, have you noticed anything out of the ordinary?"

"No. Do you want me to call the sheriff?"

Before answering Kitchi's question, Troy poked his head back inside and asked, "Is anything else missing?"

"I don't think so. Just the recorder."

The two men continued talking, but softly. Because no injuries, threats, or severe damage had occurred, they decided to keep this bothersome mischief under wraps and take care of the matter in-house.

"My main concern tonight is Ivy's safety and her state of mind. Got any ideas?"

"Too bad you don't have any dogs that could stay with her."

"Don't start with me. Getting a dog or two just leads to getting a few cats. You know *that* is never going to happen. But I do have a horse that is not fond of surprises or strangers."

They had a plan, at least for the night. Kitchi got some panels and set up a small, temporary pen just outside the cabin's only door, and with Saige's help, the cabin soon looked as if nothing out of the ordinary had occurred; she returned to her quarters. Troy stayed with Ivy until her equine guardian was in place.

Together, they stepped out to the small porch. "I'd like you to meet, Gunner. He's a great horse, though he's still a little green and has some issues with strangers. A few more months of training and he'll be fine. But tonight those issues will serve a purpose.

If anyone he doesn't know or like comes near him, he will cause quite a ruckus rearing up, screeching, and stomping. That alone should scare off any vandal. And, probably, wake you up. If that happens, press the number nine button on the cabin phone immediately. I'll have my phone next to my pillow and be here before you can say *giddyup*."

They spent the next few minutes giving Gunner some treats. "Here, see if he'll take a treat from you." Troy handed her a carrot stick, and showing her how to hold her hand flat and still. The horse wasn't fazed and almost immediately nibbled the treat from Ivy's palm, showing that he accepted and trusted her. There was hope for this wild, crazy plan.

Back inside, Ivy thanked Troy for his help and concern. "It's getting late. I guess we should call it a night and get some rest."

He gathered her in his arms, feeling responsible for what had happened. "Are you going to be okay alone? I mean, really okay?"

"Hey, I'm incredibly strong for my size and I'm not alone. I've got Gunner, remember?"

He smiled at this brave, fearless woman, and then stepped toward the door. Pausing, he turned, looking at her one final time.

"What's the matter?" she asked.

He gave no answer but walked back to her, held her face with his hands, and kissed her gently on the forehead. "Lock your door."

EXHAUSTED, sleep came easily, but it didn't last long. Disturbing dreams crept into her subconscious waking her, and although the details faded quickly, she remembered Troy had played a major roll in one of her sleepy, midnight movies.

Somewhere in that dream the number nine kept popping up, the same number she had to press to reach him on the phone in case of an emergency. According to her knowledge of numerology, the number nine was also her Life Path number. Should she read anything into that? Delve deeper into a subliminal meaning? Not tonight.

Ivy's other dream included a chorus of women chanting *Fake it till you make it* over and over. Finally, she threw up her arms in exasperation and shouted back at them, *But I'll never make it!* All the woman laughed and taunted her. She woke up shivering, covered in perspiration. Wrapping a blanket around her, she got up and peered out the window. Gunner stood calmly in the pen, relaxing one of his hind legs, so she returned to her bed hoping for a few hours of dreamless sleep before the sun came up.

The rest of the night was calm and no warnings came from the horse, she was sure of that. Being a light sleeper, any strange sounds would have woken her. Curious about her four-footed sentry, she finally got up at the break of dawn and went to the window to watch him for a few minutes before going outside. Would he still allow her to get close? Or would he become upset thinking she was a stranger? Perhaps his earlier good behavior was due to Troy's presence. She'd soon find out.

Morning wasn't far off. The darkness faded lazily, coating her surroundings in shades of dusty gray. Birds were already singing, though she couldn't actually see them. She did, however, see several horse treats on the railing of her porch. She smiled. Troy must have left them there assuming she'd try to get better acquainted with the horse. She had to admit that he'd treated her well in spite of their awkward introduction.

"Hey, Gunner, got something for you." She held out her hand the way Troy had taught her. The horse whinnied and took a few steps closer. "Come on, you can do this." She spoke calmly, delighted that he seemed to like her. He did it. He took a treat from her hand, then nudged her arm with his nose, asking for another. "All right, one more. After that, you've got to go back to work until Troy gets here."

Just as she held out her treat-filled hand, a loud BANG reverberated through the pre-dawn tranquility. Gunner spooked and jumped sideways whinnying loudly, then reared and pawed the air. Ivy dropped the rest of the treats and ran back inside. The cabin was mostly dark, strange shadows dancing with the faint morning light coming through the windows. She felt a chill go through her, a presence of some sort, but didn't stop. She had to get to the phone and call Troy.

Dashing through the main room, she grabbed the cabin phone with trembling hands and pressed the number nine button. What now? Why wasn't he answering? With her heart pounding in her ears, she waited. Still nothing. Then she remembered, this was just a signal for help. Letting go of the receiver, she turned and ran back outside.

Gunner was still agitated, whinnying loudly and darting left and right in his tight enclosure. Ivy, worried that he might get hurt, waited on the porch for Troy, ignoring the possible danger to herself. That's when she heard it, the sound of galloping hooves growing louder each second. She prayed it was Troy, but what if it wasn't?

## SEVEN

I vy recognized Tracker and the rider on his back the second they barreled around the corner of her cabin. "Troy!"

He dismounted from the unsaddled, still-moving horse, and landed on his shoeless feet. "Whoa, easy boy. You're going to be just fine." Gunner settled down almost immediately at the soothing sound of his voice. Then, stepping closer to Ivy, he asked, "What spooked him?"

"I was giving Gunner some treats, kind of a bonding moment, when a loud noise like a slamming door or a clap of thunder scared him. And me, too, for that matter."

With so little information or evidence, there was little to be done. Troy said he'd ride around the immediate area and check things out. After breakfast, Kitchi would take down the panels and walk the horse back to his stall.

Then, to her amazement, Troy leaped up onto the horse's back like a Hollywood cowboy.

"Were you a stuntman before coming to work at the ranch?"

"Nope." He winked, then flashed a smile charming enough to win any leading role. "But I'm a man of many talents." He hadn't gone far when he turned Tracker around, then trotted back. "Got any events planned for today?"

"Not yet. More sleep is high on my list, though."

"There's a moderate level hike leaving at 10:00 a.m. I'll sign you up. You'll get a wake-up call at 9:15." He looked at his watch. "You've got three hours to sleep if you go back to bed now."

Ivy nodded and turned to go inside.

"One more thing. Stop by my residence as soon as you get back from the hike, and I'll soothe your sore muscles." He took off at a gallop.

The minute her head hit the pillow, she fell into a deep, dream-filled sleep infused with pleasant visions of horses, coyotes, and all the ways Troy might soothe her aching muscles.

WOULD IVY SHOW UP? When he heard a knock on his door, he assumed it must be her. He wasn't expecting anyone else. On his way to let her in, he wondered how long she'd stay, and if she'd go along with his plan.

He opened the door and stepped aside. "Welcome to my home. Come on in," he said with a smile. "Here, let me take your sweater." She handed over the garment without hesitation, as he knew she would. The temperature inside was warm compared to the outdoor coolness.

"How was your hike? Tough enough for you?"

"Uh, yeah. You knew it would be, didn't you?"

"I knew you were a woman who enjoyed a challenge." He enjoyed the soft blush forming on her cheeks and the questioning expression visible on her face. This was the reaction he typically received, and hoped for, but unsure if he'd receive it from Ivy. He'd mentally prepared himself for rejection in case his bare chest and the tight shorts – the only item of clothing he was wearing – was not to her liking.

Now in her sleeveless blouse, jeans, and boots, she stepped closer and ran her hands from his collarbone, across his tight, ripped abs, down to his waist. Then, taking a step back, she tilted her head as if studying an ancient Greek statue, though this statue wore shorts. "I can see you're going for a comfortable, stay-at-home look this afternoon." She smiled, showing no surprise, but looking confident.

Ivy was a mystery, a puzzle that he still hadn't quite solved. Troy was confident too. There would be no rejection today. Good thing. He wouldn't know how to handle it.

It was his turn to implement the touching. He traced her lips with his fingers, then lightly stroked the entire length of her arms before raising them above her head and holding both wrists together firmly with one hand. He loved her reaction to his gentle, yet seductive move. Her eyes closed, her breathing quickened, and she groaned in anticipation. It was a good beginning, but enough for now. He needed to set his main plan for the evening in motion, so he whispered into her hear, "Can I get you something to drink?" and released her arms.

Catching her breath, she opened her eyes. "What've you got?"

"Beer, wine, champagne, tea, juice, and sparkling water. What's your pleasure, ma'am?"

She chose sparkling water. "Two sparkling waters coming up." He invited her to have a seat and rest her tired bones and over-worked muscles. She seemed preoccupied gawking at the interior of his home. A questioning frown formed on her face.

"The inside of your house is so modern, ultra modern,

while the outside looks so... rustic, like my cabin and every other building at the ranch. I don't get it, but I love it."

Troy grinned, his eyes shining. "It's all part of the experience. Guests come here for an old-fashioned, out west atmosphere, and that's what we give them. They can get 'modern' back home, any day. Now, this," he said, opening his arms wide, "is my home, and I do enjoy creature comforts as much as anyone else. Can't imagine living like a cowboy all the time if I don't have to." He smiled and, again, motioned for her to sit and relax.

"I'm good with leaning against the counter. I'm far too dusty and covered in sweat to sit on your shiny furniture."

He shook his head. "That's no surprise. I expected you'd arrive with dust. Here, come with me." Taking her hand, he led her into his bedroom.

Though she didn't say anything, he detected a tightening tension in the hand he held as they drew nearer to his king-size bed. He took pleasure in her reaction but kept on walking past the bed and into the adjoining spa, his second favorite room in the house.

"Ready to soak away your soreness?"

"I didn't bring a bathing suit," she said, raising an eyebrow. "Didn't think I'd need one. There was no mention of a pool or a spa on the ranch's website."

"No problem. Suits are optional." He stepped into the Jacuzzi and sank into the hot water. "Get in. The water's fine. I won't look unless you want me to."

Ivy pursed her lips and paused for a moment. "Okay, turn your head and close your eyes."

He turned his head only slightly and closed his eyes, but not tightly. Her hesitation surprised him, though also brought a hint of a smile to his face. "Need some help?" he offered.

"No." She seemed to search for a better answer. "Just getting used to the warmth in here."

She turned her back to him, stepped out of her hiking attire and slipped quickly into the water still wearing her silky, pink panties and bra. Troy's eyes followed every move of her nearly naked body. He'd known she was pretty right from the start, but now he knew she was far more than that. This woman in his spa was beautiful, perfectly proportioned, and physically fit.

He'd often surrounded himself with women who flaunted their assets. He wanted them to want him, even though his reciprocity always lacked emotion. That was the way he liked it. No commitments, just some good old-fashion fun, much to his parents' dismay. They wanted him to be more like Trace, his younger brother – the good brother.

Ivy sighed and closed her eyes. "This does feel great. It's been quite a while since I've been in hot water."

He laughed out loud. "I don't believe that for a minute. You began your stay at the ranch in hot water, remember?"

She scooted closer and gave his deltoid a punch. No doubt about it. That was her trademark, at least with him. This woman was different. Why didn't she swoon like all the others? Then, he saw an encouraging sign and felt confident he could change that.

She eyed him with interest, specifically his well-defined chest. Would she run her hands, now warm and wet, down the length of his chest again? With her fingers, she reached out and touched the key attached to the chain around his neck. False hope.

"This must be a very important key," she commented, then paused as if desiring an informative explanation.

Instead, he patted the key clinging to his smooth, wet skin and said, "Ah, it's the key to my heart, babe." He turned her around so she sat between his muscular legs, and massaged her shoulders.

Ivy made no attempt to move away. Troy was the first to break the closeness when the Jacuzzi jets stopped bubbling. He climbed out of the water to reset the timer, confident she'd watch his every move. Upon his return, she looked away. He looked down; his wet suit clung to his body, defining his masculinity. *I swear, sometimes this woman acts as innocent as a virgin.*

He got back in, dipped down, and then submerged completely. Resurfacing, he raked his fingers through his wet hair pushing it away from his eyes. Ivy followed his lead and went under too. Amazing. He'd never seen a female over the age of fifteen willing to ruin her hairstyle. *She doesn't mind getting her hair wet.* She came up smiling, looking naturally feminine, pretty.

The women in his past would have come up crying and dashed to find their blow dryers and make-up kits. Troy would bet money that Ivy would look great even in a windstorm, on a 5-day trail ride deep into backcountry, or mucking stalls on a rainy day. His imagination soared. This new woman was refreshing... and beautiful. Then he came to his senses. He wanted no part of refreshing and beautiful. Commitment would follow. Nope, that wasn't his life's plan.

---

IVY RELAXED and enjoyed feeling as if she were floating. The hot, bubbling water and Troy's hands massaging her shoulders were just what she'd needed. Her only thought? What would come next with this handsome cowboy?

He was a hot guy with a great job and plenty of gorgeous women vying for his attention. The fact that he'd invited her to soak in his spa didn't seem logical, but then neither did his personal residence. His place was highly impressive, too impressive, not what she'd expect for a ranch manager's dwelling.

Then, out of the blue, he said, "Times up. The pool's closing," His face wore a humorous smile. Perhaps he'd been a lifeguard in his pre-cowboy days. He sure had the body for it. Even so, his statement didn't feel right. They'd spent such a short time in the hot water, but he got right out, wrapped his lower half in a towel, and handed one to her.

Had he invited her to his spa hoping to check out her naked body? Then cut their time short because he didn't like what he saw? Possibly. He preferred the young, glamorous horsewomen, and she was neither young nor glamorous – not that twenty-nine was old – though everything about *her* body was real, natural. How many of his horsewomen could say that? She scolded herself for feeling self-conscious about her appearance and for thinking too much.

"Let yourself out when you're dressed and ready to go. Got some things I need to attend to."

The coldness in his tone was uncharacteristic. It reminded her of the moment they'd met when he'd caught her snooping around his private office. Where had his charm gone? And why?

---

TROY STRUGGLED to make sense of his actions and feelings. Why had he invited Ivy to the spa in his home and then dismissed her so rudely? She'd been sweet and spunky as always and, unlike other women, she hadn't asked him for anything. Feeling like a jerk, he kept to himself the remainder of the day, then went to bed early.

What was it about Ivy? Why was he so drawn to her? He didn't want to be. In dire need of answers, he couldn't sleep. Did she look like a past girlfriend from his impressionable and horny high school days? He searched his huge walk-in closet and found several old scrapbooks that his mother had created for him years ago, then stayed up half the night flipping through the pages.

He was about to give up on this crazy idea when he saw her. Right there, in a fragile and yellowed 1970s newspaper article – published long before he was born – was a photo of Claudine, the French singer. When he was a kid, his family watched reruns of the old Christmas specials she'd been in. God, she was gorgeous. No wonder he'd had such a crush on her. And now he had to admit that Claudine and Ivy had a similar look.

Relief swept over him. The reason for his uncharacteristic attraction to the pretty guest at his ranch was due to an unconscious memory of a childhood crush. With the mystery solved, he would finally get some sleep.

He slept, but not well. He tossed and turned dreaming of a woman skiing down a snow-covered mountain waving a gun in the air. In a flash, she'd opened the door to his bedroom and began shooting all the artwork hanging on the wall, shouting with a French accent *Take that you selfish, miserable man!*

Troy awoke from his nightmare with a cold sweat coating his body. He tried to remember his dream, but the details were vague and fading fast. Was the woman in his dream Ivy or Claudine? The answer remained elusive. Not surprising. He was just a kid when he had that crush. *Heck, maybe I do need a bodyguard – or a shrink.*

# EIGHT

The sun was up, Ivy wasn't. She lay in bed feeling sorry for herself. Running away from her medical problem was a bad idea – a weak person's action – nevertheless, here she was. But allowing a man's words shake her confidence bothered her just as much, maybe more. She didn't need a man and hadn't come here to find one.

She'd convinced herself that writing a novel would not only take her away from her stressful job but it would also make her happy. What made her think she possessed the talent required for such a lofty endeavor? Droves of thoughts rushed in. Maybe she should be a travel writer. After all, that's what she'd told Troy. *Why did I lie about that?* She'd let numerology lead her astray and right into the arms of a cowboy.

Without a doubt, coming to The Lonely Horse Ranch was a big mistake. She knew that now, though in the beginning it seemed like the perfect solution.

After chanting multiple times, *every day in every way, I'm getting better and better*, she rose from her bed, pulled on her jeans, and began her morning stroll around the ranch. Instead of her recorder, she held a small notebook with a pen clipped inside, vowing to make lemonade out of the many lemons attempting to sour her time at this beautiful place. And, if a little sleuthing was involved, so be it.

STILL DISPLEASED with himself and too mentally exhausted from his sleepless night to spend the day working in his office, Troy saddled Tracker and headed toward Big Bear Trail. They hadn't gone far when he turned his horse around and galloped back to the barn. He'd used Gunner as a safety net for Ivy but had neglected to work with him for several days. Ponying this horse-in-training up the trail behind him was the right thing to do. All three would benefit from the fresh air and solitude they'd find on this remote, all-day ride.

Troy loved the Big Bear Trail, his private trail. It meandered east of the main ranch and was deemed off-limits to guests as well as his wranglers. Today, he'd ride beyond the ranch's boundary and into national forest land.

Far from the ranch, the people, and his phone, he could be his own man and not the one his staff, the local women, or his parents wanted him to be. He'd worked hard to turn the wild, undeveloped acreage into a thriving business, though that hadn't been his lifelong dream or plan. He had no plan at all when his father turned the land over to him expecting and demanding results.

Though barely a man, once Troy opened his mind to the challenge, his vision for the land and his actions exceeded his father's demands. But he didn't do that alone. Help came along as he sat on the old, broken fence staring at the vast, sprawling land that was suddenly his. He created the Lonely Horse Ranch to please his father. He took rides into wide-open grasslands and dense forests to please himself.

Watching the autumn sun touch the hilltops, he turned the horses around and encouraged Tracker to increase his speed so they'd reach the ranch before dark. He planned for a non-stop return trip but paused to listen to an odd, howling sound. What was that? An injured or sick animal? A feral dog? The horses paid no attention to the noise, which added to the oddness and to Troy's curiosity.

He stopped, tied the horses to a tree, and took a gun

from his saddlebag in case the howling came from a rabid animal. Slowly, he approached the location where the strange noise was coming from, not wanting its source to dash away. The sound grew louder and more ear piercing as he drew closer. To his surprise, he saw the outline of a person crouched beside a leafless scrub oak bush.

"Hello? Do you need help?"

An old woman stood, and the howling stopped. Had she been the source of the odd noise? When she turned to look at Troy, her weathered appearance caused him to momentarily falter in shock. She wore tattered clothing covered with dirt; her hair looked as if it hadn't been washed or brushed in many moons; her hollow-looking face with dark, penetrating eyes stared back at him. He asked again if she needed help, although he knew the answer. He asked a different question, hoping for an informative reply. "Are you lost?"

"No, silly boy. I live here," she said, her voice gravely, her tone annoyed.

"Where is your house, your home?" he asked, his patience as thin as the light was dim, but he was curious and didn't have the heart to leave her out here alone.

The woman spread her arms straight out and spun slowly while gazing upward. Getting nowhere, Troy changed his line of questioning and quietly asked, "I heard an animal. Is it yours?"

"They're all mine. I take care of them in the summer."

"It's mid-October, ma'am. What is your name?"

She shook her head and gathered up the twigs that lay at her feet. "Mary."

"You need to go back to your winter home, Mary. Your animals will be fine."

She kept shaking her head. "No, no. Can't. There's a problem."

"I've got two horses waiting about a hundred yards from here. Stay right where you are while I get them. I'll give you a ride home. Okay?"

He thought he heard the howling a few times as he hurried back to the horses. When he returned, she was gone. "Mary? Mary! Your ride's here." He called out and rode around the area for at least thirty minutes. Finding no sign of her, he finally headed home. He'd make some inquiring calls when he got there.

The sun had set, though lingering beams of light from below the horizon gilded the gray sky. The trio would arrive at the horse barn in less than ten minutes, and although Gunner had displayed his lack of training – refusing to walk, rolling when they came to a clearing, nipping at his lead rope and a few times at Tracker's hindquarters –Troy was pleased with the horse's behavior on his first trip beyond the central portion of the ranch.

Gunner's successful day turned Troy's mood around, and he knew what he had to do next.

Looking ahead, he saw the dust just before he recognized the horse and its rider. Kitchi, his right-hand man, headed rapidly toward him. But why? The man rarely rode.

"What's up?" he asked as Kitchi's horse came to an abrupt halt beside him.

"Brought you something," he said and handed over a package.

Troy adjusted his hat and shook his head. "This couldn't wait until I got back and put up the horses?"

"Not knowing when you would return, I took it upon myself to find you."

"Well, here I am, and I need to find Ivy ASAP."

"Open the package first. One of the housekeepers found it and brought it to me."

The package contained Ivy's hand-held recorder. The sight of it brought a smile to his face. This was just what he needed to turn her mood around and be receptive to his forthcoming apology.

"Would you take Gunner back for me? I'll be in Ivy's cabin, if she's there."

Kitchi took hold of the horse's lead rope. "I suggest you listen to the words on the recorder before you proceed." His manner of speaking was often solemn, but tonight his words and his serious delivery were over the top.

Troy's patience wore thin for the second time today. "You've already listened, I take it?"

The man nodded and spoke one last word as he headed toward the barn with Gunner in tow. "Listen."

Troy found this brief conversation annoying and had to remind himself that Kitchi was not only his friend but also an intuitive, wise man. He remembered the day they'd met as if it were yesterday rather than over fifteen years ago. He'd been sitting on a rotting fence staring at a dilapidated barn and the thousands of acres of grassland and forest that were suddenly his – a gift from this father, a gift with strings attached. He'd challenged Troy to develop this property and, in the process, make something of himself.

Though glad to be away from his childhood home, The McAllister Ranch –sometimes called The Big Mack – he hadn't a clue where to begin. Then fate paid him a visit on that cold December day.

A Native American man with a black patch over one eye, wearing a backpack over a leather jacket, and holding a carved walking stick stepped toward him without making a sound. He sat on the frozen ground facing Troy. Neither spoke for quite a while. Eventually, they exchanged a few words about the weather, the land,

and opportunities. Kitchi's final words on that first day were, "You're lonely. You need a horse." They'd worked together ever since.

Troy looked down at the recording device still in his hand, and curiosity overpowered his annoyance. *What was Kitchi so concerned about? She's a writer; writers have recorders. What's the big deal?* He pushed the small PLAY button and listened.

The first few sentences answered his questions. According to her words, she'd been snooping around the ranch checking out every building, every closet, and even drawers. Troy did not like that, but he could live with it. He'd ask for an explanation when he saw her.

Troy was about to push the STOP button when her sweet voice said, "Just as I'd hoped for, I discovered an interesting safe hidden behind the portrait. Is a competitor looking for the treasure too?" *Dammit! She's a treasure hunter?*

That didn't sound like the recorded notes of a travel writer, and he felt certain such a writer wouldn't know of any hidden treasure. She was just like all the other gold-digging women though more clever and disguised in a sweet, spunky package. *Had she lied to him about her involvement with the portrait? What the hell was she up to?*

As he'd suspected earlier, she was no travel writer,

not even a *wanna-be* one. He should have trusted his gut feeling. He'd heard enough. She lied to him – he was certain of that – though he couldn't imagine why.

He'd been duped; nobody crosses Troy McAllister! He'd been a fool removing her from his list of suspects prematurely. No doubt about it. Ivy was The Lonely Horse Ranch vandal. No woman was going to use him or mess with his ranch. Furious, he wanted to confront her but rode Tracker up toward the breeding barn instead. Wisely, he took some time to cool off and come to grips with the angry words he felt compelled to shout.

NINE

Ivy refused to let anyone see her moping around, especially Troy. Putting on a heavy sweater, a swipe of mascara, and a fake smile – she was getting good at that – she headed for The Lodge to take part in the Monday Night Happy Hour. She would be happy if only for an hour.

"Hi, Ivy," Saige called from across the room, motioning for her to come closer. "What can I pour for you?"

"Got anything warm? No, make that hot! Got anything hot? It's cold out there tonight." Ivy stood in front of the bar wrapped in her own arms. She hadn't dressed warmly enough.

"Well, you're in Montana. Actually, it's been unseasonably warm this week. How about a cup of coffee topped with a swirl of Bailey's?"

"Perfect! Thanks."

Saige hummed along with the piped-in country music while preparing the drink. She turned, smiling as if she was about to hand over a precious gift. "Here you go. What do you think?"

Ivy took a few sips and sighed. "Delicious." This was exactly what she needed. "Saige, are you always so happy? You work so hard serving drinks and keeping track of the guests. Do you ever go home?"

Her question went unanswered for the moment. Another thirsty guest had stepped up to the bar. "Hello, Lester. All settled in?"

"Yes, ma'am," said the thin, older man. "And I'm ready for a beer."

"Can, bottle, or draft?"

Looking straight at Saige, never glancing at Ivy who stood only a few feet from him, he chose a can of Bud, then moved to the other side of the room.

"Who was that guy?" Ivy inquired. "I haven't seen him around or at meals."

"It was the weirdest thing. He just dropped in today. Had no reservation. That never happens. We're kind of off the beaten path. Nobody just drives by and stops in." She shrugged. "This time of year, when the weather turns chilly but there's still no snow, we sometimes have an unoccupied room. He got lucky."

Ivy eyed the man with curiosity. There was something about him that tickled her mind, but she didn't know what. "Back to my prying question. Do you ever go home?"

"I love this place. This is my home. My only home. It's Kitchi's home too. I rarely leave unless Troy or a guest requires something from town. Being here is like... a forever vacation."

Hearing that Saige lived here full-time came as a surprise to Ivy. She'd assumed most of the employees, except Troy and several wranglers, went home at the end of the day. New questions arose.

"How long have you lived and worked here?"

Saige looked as if she was calculating her answer. "Almost ten years. Kitchi was Mr. McAllister's first hire. He's been here the longest, but that is not my story to tell."

"Can you tell me about the patch over his eye?"

"No, I can't. I know nothing about that and neither does Troy." She refilled Ivy's cup as additional thirsty guests filed in. "Talk to you later."

Sipping her drink and nibbling on delicious, unusual snacks she could not name, Ivy glanced around the room. No sign of Troy. That suited her just fine. She hadn't come to the ranch to find a man, she'd come in search of a story, a story that might mention one or more of these tasty treats. She'd ask Kitchi about the ingredients tomorrow. Her hunger satisfied, she felt no need to stick around for dinner.

Back in her cabin, Ivy sat at the small table by the window angry with herself on several counts. First, that she'd left her recorder in the cabin the night of the cookout after promising to keep it with her at all times. If she had, it wouldn't be missing and she'd be transcribing her spoken thoughts right now. Second, she'd allowed herself to have romantic feelings for a man, a cowboy no less. And third, she thought he had romantic feelings for her. Number three bothered her the most.

*Lessons learned. Do what you came here to do.* Ivy could be tough on herself. She often was, and tonight was no exception. She felt her skin growing thicker, as it did when she was on the job back in Denver. Previous thoughts and new words tumbled out directly from her brain to the page. No recorder acting as the middleman was needed. She doodled stick figures between brilliant thoughts. She was on a roll, in a zone – the author zone. Maybe she could write a book after all. She removed the 'maybe' and repeated her thought.

Ivy stared down at the five pages of messy writing and was delighted with her accomplishment when the approaching sound of a horse's galloping hooves broke her concentration. Her logical mind thought it odd since all trail rides returned before dusk. Except for Gunner, she'd never seen any horses out at night. Something must have happened. Something bad.

Peering out into the dim, evening light, she saw Troy and Tracker speeding toward her cabin, and one of them looked angry. Throwing his leg over the saddle even before Tracker had come to a full stop, Troy slid off. He must need her help. Apparently, a serious matter had come up. Deciding to meet him halfway, she went outside.

"What's wrong? What happened?"

He raised the hand holding her recorder. "Look what turned up."

Joy, pure joy bubbled up inside her. Casting aside the second and third reasons for her recent angry feelings, the words 'thank you' sprung from her lips and her arms reached out to hug the recorder's rescuer.

Troy pushed her away. "I don't know who you are or what you're doing here, but you'll pack your bags because the day after tomorrow you're leaving the ranch. Your two-week vacation has been whittled down to one." He ranted on and on, not letting her say much of anything.

Caught off guard, no intelligent response came to

Ivy's mind, just an angry one. "You listened to the words on my recorder?"

Scowling, he nodded stiffly.

"Does that mean you won't bring Gunner here tonight?" Her question, despite the bad timing, was sincere.

Troy's red-hot anger turned icy cold. He shook his head, pointing his finger right at her. "Did you not hear anything I've said? *You* are the vandal. You're the problem around here. What am I supposed to do? Protect you from... yourself? Nice little stunt, trashing your own cabin. I should have known from the first time we met that you were one crazy female."

"I would never do anything to hurt you or the—"

"Enough! We're done," he seethed, and the turned to face Tracker. Without looking back, Troy grabbed the saddle horn, swiftly swung himself into the seat, and rode away faster than he'd arrived.

Alone now, her immediate reaction was to wonder if he really had the power to kick out a paying guest. He wasn't the owner, after all. She felt terrible. *Let me count the ways.* No, she'd play no additional number games tonight. Instead, she sat down on the front porch and listened to the words and phrases saved on her recorder. Yeah, she could see how he might have misinterpreted her intentions.

## TEN

After a restless night fraught with one of his recurring nightmares about cats – Troy hated cats: big ones, small ones, it didn't matter – he lay in bed longer than usual. He noticed the sunlight penetrating the majestic pines standing tall to the east of his residence, streaming through his window, creating designs on his bedroom wall. If Ivy were here, she'd talk or write about the wall art provided by Mother Nature.

That unwanted thought brought him to his feet. All he needed now was a strong cup of coffee to sustain his vertical momentum and keep his uncomfortable emotions concerning Ivy at bay.

Kitchi must have seen him coming. A cup of coffee, just the way he liked it, was ready for him. "Morning,

Troy," he said. "Glad you stopped by. We were just talking about the new guy."

"What new guy?"

Saige was ready with her two-cents. "Lester. He checked in yesterday afternoon."

"Is there a problem with Lester?" Troy needed to know. His staff rarely gossiped about a guest.

"No, but he's odd and seems out of place, that's all. Doesn't say much," Kitchi said.

Saige seemed to know him best. "His registration paperwork was kind of vague, and he had no interest in signing up for any activities. Why be here if you don't take part in what the ranch has to offer?"

"He might just need time away from his current life situation. Everybody needs to get away now and then." Troy thanked them for the update and said he'd be making his usual rounds. Later in the day, when Saige was alone, he'd let her know about Ivy's early departure. She might need help rescheduling her new travel arrangements.

Cody, the head wrangler, left with him. "Just thought you'd like to know that Ivy left early this morning on an all-day, nose-to-tail trail ride. Said she'd never ridden a horse before." He laughed. "She's gonna be hurting this afternoon. Later, boss."

Troy led Tracker to the large pasture north of the

barn. The horse deserved a day of rest. He'd make his rounds on foot this morning, and that would help work off some steam. First stop, the main arena. One of the women's riding groups would be practicing their moves by now. As usual, seeing them lifted his spirits and was good for his ego. He got the expected attention, stayed longer than usual, then moved on to the wranglers' bunkhouse.

He shook his head at the disarray. These cowboys needed a lesson in picking up after themselves. Being men didn't give them a license to be sloppy. A quick check in the barn and the main tack room was next. Then he'd stop by his place for a protein shake before heading to his private gym.

It was noon by the time he returned to his residence. Right away, he sensed something was different. Nothing obvious at first, but on closer inspection, several items were out of place and a few drawers were not closed properly. Always meticulous about the order and arrangement of his possessions, he concluded someone besides his housekeeper had been there. But who, and why?

It could not have been Ivy. She was sitting on the back of a horse somewhere on Pine Meadows Trail. Putting together a short, mental timeline, he was certain she wasn't this morning's intruder. And maybe she wasn't the vandal of her own cabin either. *Dammit.*

He'd go pump some iron while he waited for the trail riders and Ivy to return. A second apology was in order – unless she had an accomplice.

---

THE HORSES AMBLED toward the hitching post in a straight line ready for a drink of water and some oats. Ivy spotted Troy looking directly at her. He wouldn't dare show his anger in front of the other riders, would he?

She observed one of the wranglers making his way down the line of horses helping riders dismount. Impatient and wanting nothing more than to lie down on the bed in her cabin, she took her feet out of the stirrups, swung her leg over the horse, and slid to the ground. To her complete surprise, her knees buckled under her and she landed on her butt, embarrassed.

"I've got this one," Troy said to the closest wrangler, then scooped Ivy up in his arms.

Was he suppressing a laugh or hiding his irritation? She couldn't tell. His face wore an expression she hadn't seen before. What were his intentions? She felt like a rag doll as he carried her toward the water trough. She stiffened and closed her eyes, bracing for the cold dunking.

"We need a do-over."

Her eyes opened wide. "A do-over? What are we doing over?"

"Everything." He set her down gently. "Do you think you can walk now?"

"Yes." Her knees hurt, but she was determined to walk on her own. "Where are we going?"

Looking straight ahead, he took her hand. "To my place."

They walked in silence. Troy, with confidence; Ivy, with suspicion. He no longer seemed angry, so what was he up to? His motive became clear as he led her straight through his bedroom to the spa. Was this cowboy in dire need of seeing a naked woman? If so, that need would go unfulfilled.

"I know you must be hurting. A good soak will help that."

"No. No way am I getting—" He handed her a bathing suit. "Oh, I get to wear this?" Sarcasm slithered out. "Am I the fifth, the tenth, or the twentieth woman to wear it?"

"You're the first."

Her distrusting smirk melted away when she noticed the sales tag hanging from the shoulder strap. She *was* the first.

Troy's suggestion that she change into the suit in the privacy of the master bathroom pleased her until she gave his statement a quick thought. *He doesn't want to see me naked.* Was that a step in the right direction? Part of his do-over plan? Or a let's-just-be-friends thing?

The suit was not bad looking and it almost fit. A soak would feel good. He was right about that. Taking a few deep, cleansing breaths, she returned to the spa expecting to see Troy in the water. Instead, she found him wearing a Speedo-type suit and organizing items on the spa's shelves. He looked up and smiled.

"I can't help it. Some say that neatness is my most annoying flaw."

Neatness, to a point, was good in her book. "Thanks for the suit. Let's soak."

Ivy closed her eyes. She'd had no idea that sitting on the back of a horse all day would be so tiring and, at the ride's end, so painful. They soaked in silence on opposite sides of the tub. The hot water and bubbling jets soothed her mind as well as her body. Ah, heaven!

Relaxed and sleepy, she mumbled, "Have you met the new guest, Lester?"

"Saige mentioned him, but I haven't seen him. Why do you ask?"

She knew she was biting her lip. A habit she detested. "No reason. Just wondered." Her eyes returned to the closed position until Troy's hands held her face.

"Ivy, I jumped to conclusions. It was wrong to accuse

you of vandalizing your own cabin, snooping around, and talking trash about the ranch on your recorder. I over-reacted, and I'm sorry about that. Can we start over?"

With newfound energy, she wrapped her arms around his neck and crossed her legs around his waist.

"I'm going to take that as a yes," he said, smiling.

"For your information," she paused, clearing her throat, then snapped her fingers and sang, "All my bags are packed, I'm ready to go. I'm soaking here…" She paused, biting her lower lip again, her eyes wide with expectation. He'd said he was sorry, but did he still want her to leave? She had been snooping, looking for signs of treasure.

"Yeah. About that. Unpack your bags. Stay. In fact, I'll tack on a few extra days to your vacation. How does that sound?" Troy didn't wait for her answer. He traced her lips with his finger before tickling them with his tongue. Covering her mouth with his, they continued the kiss under water. A whole new experience for Ivy, possibly for Troy too.

Though sensual, the underwater kiss had its limits, and they rose up in need of air. With their lungs replen-ished with oxygen, the kissing began again. This time, above water. Troy lifted one of her legs exposing her knee. He kissed it, then massaged it gently. It hurt so good. He'd begun the same wonderful process on the other knee when his cell phone rang. Giving her a peck on the cheek, he said, "Don't go away."

His phone lay on one of the spa shelves, so Ivy watched him answer it. To be more precise, she stared at him as he spoke. The man was too good-looking. Every inch of him was firm, tan, and ripped. How was it possible that a cowboy had the physique of a slim, chiseled bodybuilder? You don't get that from riding a horse or telling stories around a campfire.

So far, all he'd said was 'Troy here.' Though, a few seconds later he turned, looked right at her, and shook his head. He spoke a few more words into the phone and finished with, "I'll be right there." He was dressed before she'd dried off. "Let yourself out, okay?"

With a gloomy sense of déjà vu, she dressed and returned to her cabin.

———

JOGGING ALL THE WAY, not completely dry and still fastening the snaps on his shirt, Troy entered the bunkhouse out of breath, but ready to handle the situation whatever it might be.

"So, where is this problem that can't wait?" Annoyance coated his words.

Cody looked perplexed. "Are you kidding me, Troy?

This has always been the plan, *your* plan, whenever I know you have a female visitor in your home."

In the past, Cody provided Troy with an escape route from women that lingered too long. They had a deal. More often than not, he did want to cut short his rendezvous with women before they got too comfortable or assumed they could spend the night in his bed.

"Dammit. I forgot."

Now, Cody looked annoyed. "You forgot? Well, son-of-a-gun. That's a first."

"A lot of firsts going on around here lately. It's not your fault. I was kind of in the middle of something. Something good. And I just wasn't thinking." He kicked a small rock and stomped off to his locked barn, his private sanctuary.

Ignoring the snaps on his shirt, he lifted it over his head, exposing his chest to the barn's chilly temperature. He could have switched on the heater, but he was too preoccupied with thoughts of Ivy to feel the cold. Wearing only his jeans and boots, he pumped some iron, broke a sweat, and devised a plan. Tomorrow, he'd take Ivy on a picnic if she'd agree to go with him. After leaving her alone in his spa on two separate occasions, that was a big IF.

# NAKED BULL RIDING, PUPPY LOVE, & THE WOODLAND POWWOW

ELEVEN

At breakfast, without saying a word, Kitchi handed Ivy an envelope and hurried back to the kitchen. "Thanks," she called after him. Slipping it under her plate, she continued chewing the mouthwatering scrambled eggs. She was hungry, ravenous actually. The contents of the envelope could wait until after she'd eaten.

Her curiosity wasn't so easily put on hold, though. Between bites of bacon, fruit, and more eggs, her imagination swung from good to bad like a fortune-telling pendulum. Perhaps the envelope contained an apology from Troy for leaving so abruptly last night, or it could be a plane ticket for an early flight back to Denver. He'd threatened to send her home early once before.

Not wanting to receive any news, good or bad, in the presence of the other guests, she hurried back to her cabin. Sitting on the porch, she opened the envelope and unfolded the note. It was GOOD news! Troy apologized but gave no explanation for his sudden departure. That was okay. There was more. The good news was followed by great news. He'd pick her up at ten o'clock. They were going on a picnic together.

She made a mental note not to ask about the problem that took him from their cozy spa time yesterday, though she wanted to. Ranch business was none of her business. And, they weren't in a relationship. Not really. She could tell he wasn't in the market for that. She was his flavor of the month. He was her escape-from-reality fling. Just as well.

Once he discovered her physical limitations, he'd lose interest anyway. A man as sexy and virile as Troy would definitely want the exact thing she couldn't give him.

She listened for the sound of horses' hooves, assuming they'd be riding the animals to the picnic location. Instead, she heard the noise of an engine as Troy drove up on an off-road quad.

"Your chariot awaits, my dear. Hop in."

She took one long look at the coolers, the blankets, and several unidentified metal containers strapped down in the back of the vehicle, and climbed aboard. "The chariot is well-packed. Are we going on a three-day picnic?"

"I like to be prepared for anything. Locked and loaded. You never know what might come along on the far side of a Montana ranch."

"And everything is strapped down because...?"

His smile contained mischief. "It's going to be a bumpy ride. You'd better buckle up."

"Don't tell me you haven't maintained your dirt road," she teased playfully.

Revving the engine, he sped off and shouted, "There is no road, not even a trail. What fun would that be?"

Ivy quickly fastened her seatbelt and prepared mentally for Mr. Toad's Wild Ride. Speed didn't bother her, she'd had plenty of exposure to traveling fast, but only on paved, level roads. The ride in the off-road quad, driven by a cowboy, promised a different kind of excitement.

The warmth of the midday sun directly above them offset the wind chill factor induced by the swift and bumpy movement of the vehicle. Though Ivy loved the feeling of the wind tousling her hair, she wished Troy would slow down enough for her to study and enjoy the beautiful landscape. How could she come up with descriptive words if all she saw was a blur?

As if a mind reader, Troy cut the engine and coasted

slowly down the slight hill. Were they sneaking up on something? Or was there an unforeseen mechanical problem? She was about to ask when he put a finger to his lips. Ivy's eyes looked from side to side and she shrugged.

He knew something that she had not yet figured out. He pointed off to the right, and there it was. A huge, deerlike animal. They sat in silence watching it graze before it ambled back into a dense grove of trees. "Well, princess, you just met a Royal."

"A Royal? It looked like a big deer to me."

"That 'deer' was a six-point bull. An elk. A Royal. Later in the afternoon, he'll be actively looking for a few girlfriends. We'll need to keep our distance then. He'll want some alone time, if you know what I mean." Troy winked at her and chuckled.

"No, cowboy, not sure that I do. Want to explain?"

"Just thinking how nice a little alone time with you would be," he replied with an innocent shrug.

He placed his hand on her thigh, giving it a pat and a squeeze. The stillness – between the shrill cries of a pair of hawks circling above – filled Ivy's heart and soul with joy. Basking in the moment, she vowed to remember this peaceful, easy feeling forever.

Quiet time over, the engine roared again. They

bounced up a rather steep hill, getting temporarily stuck a time or two. Troy's muscles bulged as he gripped the steering wheel and sweat formed on his face in spite of the cool, outdoor temperature. Ivy, needing more than her seatbelt, hung tightly to the handhold located on the console between her and Troy. At the top of the rise, he announced, "We're here! Are you hungry?"

"As soon as my body stops vibrating and my stomach settles down, I will be." Mesmerized by the awesome, 360-degree view, she hadn't noticed that Troy had left her side. The sudden silence produced a bothersome ringing in her ears forcing her to close her eyes and cover her ears with her hands. Her actions didn't help much. A few minutes later, the pleasant chirping of birds, lots of birds, replaced the ringing sound.

She jerked in surprise when Troy unlatched the quad's door. He led her to a blanket and a spread of food waiting to be devoured. Food that looked more like a gourmet feast than a picnic.

"Wow! Kitchi has outdone himself today."

"Nope. It wasn't Kitchi. He's a good ranch cook, but he doesn't prepare food like this. I do." He seemed quite proud of himself. "I hope you like the tomato focaccia and the potato and pepper phyllo cups. For dessert, we have cherry and cream cheese finger pies."

Was she more intrigued by the fancy, unfamiliar food set out before her, or the fact it had been prepared by a cowboy? She couldn't decide.

"I'm having my usual drink: a Seven and Seven. What can I pour for you? I brought Riesling, soda, and sparkling water."

"Since you're drinking, I will too. The Riesling sounds wonderful."

Heaven couldn't be much better than this. A high mountain meadow, a to-die-for meal, and Troy. She could get used to— No, no, no! She put a stop to her ridiculous and impossible thoughts. In less than a week, she'd be back in Denver working the eleven to seven shift if she still had a job and spending lonely nights pretending to be a writer.

Still, she hoped he would embrace her, pull her tightly to him, and kiss her long and deep. Who was she kidding? She wanted more than that. She wanted to be Troy's woman if only for the duration of her stay. She'd worry about leaving and saying goodbye later.

A gentle breeze played with the loose strands of her hair, and she closed her eyes. A delicious pine scent tickled her nose. Was that scent from a nearby tree? Or Troy? She knew the answer. The man smelled too darn good. He sat behind her, surrounding her with his arms, and nibbled at her neck. Would he make love to her on this mountain? Did she want to go that far? It could complicate things, making future decisions more distressing.

She had no illusions of being his one and only but taking unnecessary risks of the heart was not her thing – thinking too much was. Her immediate thought made her blush. She'd sampled his excellent cooking skills, but if he offered her a sample of his lovemaking, would she take it?

Sitting face to face on the thick blanket, his fingers inched her blouse to the side exposing her shoulder to the afternoon sun and taking her breath away. For the first time, she saw a genuine tenderness in his gaze, a look as soft as a caress. She melted in the comfort of his nearness as he unbuttoned her blouse and tossed it to the side.

He'd seen her wearing nothing but underwear once before, so why did she feel completely undressed with the mere removal of her shirt? Her pretty pink bra still covered her breasts. Her heart thumped erratically, jump-starting her long suppressed passion, and she began to unbutton his shirt. She took her time, kissing his chest each time she moved lower to the next button.

She moaned softly as he lay her down and brushed a gentle kiss across her forehead. "You're one of a kind, Ivy. I'm not sure what to do."

She put her arms around his neck. "What do you want to do?"

"I want to take you, ravish you, and give you pleasure like you've never had before." He looked worried, upset, even unsure. His mixed message confused her. "None of my past sexual encounters included deep feelings. I can do sex, no problem. Sex combined with deep feelings? That's new territory for me."

She appreciated his candor and had already figured out that despite his storytelling showmanship and his flirting with the horseback-riding women, he was a loner – with an ego, too cool to fail.

She spoke the first words that came to mind. "Shut up and kiss me."

He laughed and said, "Yes, ma'am. That, I can do."

Their playful kisses quickly converted into hot and heavy petting. He moved his mouth over hers, devouring its softness. She returned his kisses with reckless abandon, each pausing to catch their breath. The breeze, the birds, everything around them became profoundly silent as if time stood still. Ivy couldn't decide if that was eerie or heavenly. Then, a faint noise drifted by, and her thinking shifted.

She whispered, "Troy, did you hear that?" Though her question had poor timing, she couldn't ignore the odd, moaning sound. "Troy!"

Emerging from his spellbound state, he heard it too. The rancher in him took over. "We've got to check it out." She'd never seen him move so quickly. They left everything where it lay and dashed shirtless to the quad.

# TWELVE

Now she worried, not about the leaving, but the drive down the steep hill that felt more like flying, an activity she avoided whenever possible. Troy veered the quad to the west, cut the engine, and listened. The sound was louder. The faint moaning of one had been replaced by the loud bellowing and screeching of several. They were headed in the right direction.

Moving swiftly on the semi-level, rocky surface, Troy shouted, "Get the gun from the compartment in front you. One way or another, we're going to need it."

"What are we looking for?" Ivy's heart raced as she surveyed the surrounding terrain.

In a split second, they both knew the answer. Troy grabbed the gun from her hand and shot into the air. A mountain lion stood its ground, looked up from its injured prey, and let loose a high pitched, short roar before hissing at the quad they sat in. The cow continued to bellow, but her blood-soaked calf was too quiet. He handed the gun back to Ivy, needing both hands on the wheel.

Troy, his face pale, his hands shaking, revved the engine, blasted the horn, and drove erratically, not wanting to provide the angered animal an alternate tasty target. Ivy shouted and, shocking herself, pulled the trigger a few times. Eventually, their combined efforts were more than the big cat wanted to deal with, and it bounded up and over the hill.

When they drove closer, Troy saw the red tag on the cow's ear and said she was one of his. "I'm surprised she and her calf were up at this altitude so late in the season." He found a rope and, with shaky hands, tied one end around the cow's neck, the other to the back of the quad. She'd be following them to the ranch.

"Are we still on ranch land?"

"No, we're on national forest land." His voice wavered, and he kept looking over his shoulder.

He'd saved his cow and ran the mountain lion off. He should feel good, so what was bothering him? The calf, of course. In all the excitement, she'd forgotten about the poor thing.

"Leave it, Ivy. It's either already dead or too far gone to save. We need to get away from here."

She ignored his command and went to see for herself. She couldn't find a pulse through the animal's thick fur and skin, but it was breathing. "I need your pants, Troy. Hurry."

He stood there, confusion apparent on his face, trying to make sense of her request. But it was taking too long for him to react and the calf wouldn't survive much more blood loss.

Without missing a beat, Ivy stood and removed her jeans. "The gashes look deep. Got an extra blanket or clean rags? I need fabric, something, anything. Got to put together some make-do bandages."

Troy glanced back at the quad and shook his head. They'd left everything at the picnic area. Ivy nodded and continued her efforts to save the calf. Time was of the essence. She stopped the bleeding on its neck as much as possible by wrapping her jeans around it and applying pressure, then used her belt as a tourniquet on its front leg.

"Troy, get some water."

He shook his head. "You're wasting your time. I'm telling you, it's too far gone."

"Please. Water. Hurry!"

He nodded and brought over the five-gallon container

that had been strapped to the back of the quad. Fascinated, he watched the nearly topless, jean-less city girl clean the calf's wounds, stop the bleeding, and get it to drink some water. "Why isn't it moving?"

"Give her some time. She's in shock. It's a good thing we got here when we did."

Ivy suggested that Troy drive the quad and the cow over closer. Reluctantly, he complied with her request. The cow nuzzled her calf, and the calf lifted its head.

"What do think this little girl weighs?"

"I'm guessing a hundred pounds, give or take a few. Why are you asking?"

"So we'll know how much we're lifting." She laughed at the horrified look on his face.

"I'm more of a businessman, a money guy, a storyteller. I love the ranch and all its animals, but I'm not a cow-lifting guy."

"You are now. I can't do this by myself."

Between the two of them, they managed to load the calf into the back of the quad. The evidence of their romantic picnic would remain where they'd left it for now. Troy wanted to make sure they arrived at the ranch before sundown.

"Our journey back to the ranch needs to be as slow as a snail's pace. The calf can't take too many bumps. Okay?"

Troy nodded. "I got this."

Neither spoke for a while though the cow and calf communicated a bit.

"You were great back there, Ivy. I'm really impressed." He placed a hand on her thigh, and a new ah-ha came to mind. "Wait. You're a veterinarian, aren't you?"

She felt good, talented, and in dire need of some clothing. "No, and don't be silly. That was nothing. Just some basic first aid anyone could do."

"I don't think so. You were fearless in the presence of a mountain lion. You shot a gun and ran toward a large, frightened mother cow! And then, as if nothing in the world could stop you, you took care of the calf and slowed down the bleeding. I could go on and on. Come on, Ivy, who are you, really?"

Was he still complimenting her cow-saving deeds, or was he eyeing her with suspicion again? Her arms crossed, covering her chest, she couldn't remember ever being this cold. Not even in Denver in the winter. Turning to watch the cow and her calf, Ivy smiled. "We're quite a sight, huh?"

"We sure are," he said, driving slower than an elderly snail. He brought the quad to a complete stop, leaned toward her, and kissed her lovingly on the lips.

---

IVY SHIVERED with chill and fatigue, but never once complained. Troy wished he had a shirt to wrap around her, but his shirt was back with hers at the picnic spot. He wished he could hurry, but that wasn't possible either. Slow and easy was the only way.

"I don't remember seeing that bell-shaped rock formation or crossing any streams on our way to the picnic," she said and looked around with concern.

"Good observation. You are correct, because we didn't." He began to whistle a tune to avoid further discussion on that topic.

"We're not lost, right?"

"Nope. Just taking a different route home."

"And why is that?"

He let out a long sigh. His avoidance tactic had failed. He'd hoped she wouldn't ask that question. Should he give her an honest answer? Or one she might prefer to hear? Who was he kidding? Ivy was a strong woman, and when it came to anything involving cats, she'd proved her toughness, her absence of fear.

"Would you accept 'because' as my answer?" He knew she wouldn't. He was stalling. He braced himself for one of her deltoid punches on his bare skin. No punch came, instead, she appeared to be deep in thought.

"We're in danger, aren't we?"

"I'm just covering the bases and taking precautions. What's that term you city gals use? Oh, yeah. I'm being proactive."

"Regarding?"

He sighed. "The mountain lion. To him, we are a traveling gourmet meal that would feed him for several weeks, and we carry with us the strong scent of fresh blood."

Troy explained that he'd chosen this route because it was shorter and would get them home sooner, even at this slow pace. Also, he was confident the big cat was less likely to come this way as it carried the scent of many horses and riders left from daily trail rides.

Ivy seemed satisfied with the truth and took it upon herself to be the lookout, scanning the terrain for the cat or any other possible danger. Eventually, they stopped to offer the calf and the cow some water. The cow's mooing had a contented tone, no longer afraid or stressed. The calf was doing well also. Almost too well. It attempted to stand in the back of the quad several times.

Troy took off his cowboy hat, shook his head, and pushed his hair back. "We can't let him do that. He'll hurt himself or tip over the quad."

"He? He's a baby bull?" For some reason, unknown to Troy, she was delighted that the calf was a baby bull.

"Yes, so far, that's what he is. He'll be a steer before long."

"We can't let him walk, he's too weak, and without an x-ray, I can't be sure about the damage done to his front leg."

"I could put it out of its misery."

"No! I've got a better idea."

It was dusk by the time they arrived back at the ranch. The guests had finished their evening meal and were either enjoying after dinner drinks in the bar or the quiet of their own rooms or cabins.

Fortunately, this time of year the only after dark, outdoor activity occurred on Friday. Troy and Ivy breathed a sigh of relief that their return had gone unnoticed. The little caravan would look bizarre, even frightening, to almost anyone who saw it.

What a sight. Two nearly naked adults covered in blood and towing a cow behind an off-road quad. And that was the good part. Ivy's idea? She sat in the back with the baby bull's head in her lap as she stroked him, talked to him, and now and then sat on him to keep him from standing. The plan was to park at Troy's place and quickly throw on some clothing – anything would do – before dealing with the calf and cow. And it would have worked if Kitchi hadn't come riding up.

"Dammit!" It seemed whenever Troy screwed up,

Kitchi was nearby shaking his head. He had to admit this did appear to be a major screw-up. "Kind of late to be out riding, don't you think?" That was all Troy could come up with.

"I was concerned when you hadn't returned by sunset." He chuckled, still shaking his head.

Troy asked Kitchi to drive the quad and take the cow to the empty stall in the horse barn, then get Cody or Willy to help him lift the calf and place it in with its mother. The animals would be safe there until morning.

"I'll ride your horse back to its stall, Kitchi." The two men traded places.

Kitchi, now sitting in the quad with the cow in tow, had a few last words. "If I'd known, Miss Ivy, that you'd be taking up naked bull riding, I'd have been looking for you much sooner."

After shaking his head and sending a humorous glare Kitchi's way, he turned toward Ivy and said, "Our plan to throw *on* some clothing – is off. I'll be right back." He winked and galloped away.

IVY WENT straight to Troy's shower to wash the dirt and the calf's blood from her shivering body. The hot water cascading down from four separate showerheads drenching every inch of her was just what she needed. She dried off with a towel as large as a throw blanket, then, feeling certain he wouldn't mind, found a t-shirt in one of his drawers and put it on. What remained of her clothing was currently unwearable.

Without the cowboy here watching her every move, she noticed the extreme neatness of his home's master bedroom and bath area. Every t-shirt was perfectly folded and stacked with precision. The clothes in his closet all hung in the same direction, arranged by type and color. He had to be neatest ranch manager in the entire world. The thought brought a smile to her face.

Troy would be back soon, and she wanted to be ready. Three delightful ideas came to mind. First, she found two non-breakable wine glasses in his well-equipped kitchen, filled them with red wine, and carried them to the spa. There she figured out how to work his surround sound system and selected a Keith Urban disc from his collection to play. She paused before implementing her third idea. Did she dare?

She'd provide *turndown* service for him and let him decide how to interpret such an action. If only she had a piece of chocolate to place on his pillow. Halfway to the kitchen, she heard the sound of a quad and assumed it was Troy coming home. She hurried to the spa area where she'd wait for him.

Ivy heard the door close and the sound of his foot-steps as he made his way toward the bedroom. Soon, he stood in the spa's doorway looking like the muddied-up cowboy she'd met her second day on the ranch.

"You've been busy," he said, smiling. "Hang on, cowgirl, I've got some catching up to do."

While he showered, she turned on the music and dimmed the lights. He returned wearing a towel and an even bigger smile. "You got anything on besides my t-shirt?"

She shook her head. "I didn't think it was appropriate for me to wear your shorts."

"I see." He stepped closer and pulled the t-shirt over her head. Once she was able to lower her arms, she removed his towel. Hand in hand they slipped into the hot water together.

Ivy lifted the wine glasses ready to make a toast about their unbelievable adventure. Troy reached for one of the drinks, then stood up in the swirling water. "I'll be right back."

Surprised, all she could say was, "Okay."

He returned in a couple of minutes.

"So, share. What's going on?" she asked.

He wiggled his eyebrows up and down. "You'll know soon enough."

What could she do? Shrugging, she slipped deeper

into the water. Side by side, up to their chins in hot water, they sipped the wine, listened to the music, and nearly fell asleep.

"Come on, babe. Let's hit the hay."

After drying off, he led her to his bed. A chocolate truffle topped each pillow. *Perhaps great minds do think alike.* Ivy was too tired to eat the chocolate, but she loved the gesture and mumble, "Thank you."

They fell asleep the moment their heads hit the pillows.

## THIRTEEN

Troy slept well. He attributed the restful night to the beautiful woman who lay under the covers by his side. Almost two days without any vandalism, misplaced items, or disturbing nightmares might have played a role too. And, there was the sheer exhaustion from yesterday's picnic, saving the cows, and the threat of the mountain lion that likely contributed to his uninterrupted deep sleep.

It was still very early, just after dawn. Not wanting to disturb Ivy, he slowly and quietly slipped out of bed. He would take full advantage of his excess energy and complete the day's self-appointed tasks in record time, tackling the paperwork first. Not that he enjoyed it or was required to do it. He had people for that.

Saige kept accurate records of the costs and income

associated with guest housing. Kitchi did the same for everything food related, as Cody did for the cattle, the barns, and the trail horses. Even so, Troy always took a weekly look at the numbers. An accountant in town kept the official books based on the good work of these key staff members.

Troy's baby was the horse-breeding component at the ranch. That part of the business was off limits to others. Only his eyes, the accountant, and the IRS were privy to those numbers, not that he had anything to hide. In the beginning, he'd wanted to give horse breeding a try simply to prove to himself and his dad that he could make a go of it. After only a few years, he fell in love with his horses, the breeding, and the birthing process – not to mention the big bucks that rolled in. Since then, he'd kept that 'little slice of heaven' pretty much to himself.

Was it the hands on the antique clock or the growl of his stomach that got his attention? Either way, he left his office to begin his daily rounds of the property and all the buildings. First stop, the dining hall. He grabbed a sandwich and said hello to the guests. Only twenty dined in today. Twelve others were on a trail ride, and eight were on a hike. All had sack lunches with them.

Troy heard singing as he approached the kitchen door.

"Singing? You're singing today?" Kitchi was a peaceful, contented man, but outwardly happy? No. Troy hadn't witnessed that emotion before, and they'd worked together for many years.

"I suppose I am. I'd whistle, but I'm not good at that." Kitchi turned his back to Troy and removed a large tray of cookies from the oven.

Troy, though curious, was at a loss for words. "Hmm. Want to explain?"

"No. Did you like the sandwich of the day?"

"It was different. And, yes, I liked it."

Kitchi, comfortable with his standard fare, rarely tried new recipes. "Had some help. Here take these cookies out to the folks." Troy chuckled. Something was going on here. He took the tray of cookies to the dining hall, set it down, and headed toward the door.

One guest called out, "Did our little darlin' give you your number yet?"

Not wanting to insult a guest or make himself look uninformed, he said, "Nope. Not yet." Before he'd reached the exit, another guest added, "She's such a sweet heart, loving all God's creatures like she does. Even that creepy little thing."

*What the heck is going on around here?* First, Kitchi singing and trying new recipes, then a guest asking about his number. Maybe he was more uninformed and out of touch than he imagined, but that would change before the sun set that evening.

No other odd comments came his way during the remainder of his rounds, and with his work done for the day, Troy headed toward the pasture where Tracker often hung out in the morning. That's when he noticed Ivy sitting on the top rail of the corral talking to one of the horses. "How's that conversation going?"

She turned. "Sarcasm will get you nowhere, Mr. Bigshot. Besides, I'm talking to myself. It's not my fault the horse is listening and responding." She raised her eyebrows just like one of his elementary teachers used to do. That was not a look he wanted to receive from the beautiful woman he'd slept naked with last night.

Holding up her recorder, she said, "Keeping track of my thoughts and ideas. And now I've got your *how's that conversation going* on tape too." She added that the barn coat she wore home was at her cabin and she'd return it to him later today.

Troy wondered what triggered the increase in her spunkiness. He didn't mind, though. In fact, he enjoyed that part of her personality. She was nothing like those flirty women who constantly vied for his attention. At times, it seemed like she didn't want his attention. If she was consciously playing hard to get, her strategy was working. *Game on, Miss Ivy.*

"Since you're wearing jeans, and I see you've found a shirt of your own to put on, how about going for a short, easy trail ride with me?" When she hesitated, he added more temptation to his offer. "We could swing by the western pasture and check on your calf? I know for a fact that's where it is right now."

"When do we leave?"

"Just as soon as we get our horses saddled up." He led her to the grassy pasture that adjoined the corral. "I'm riding Tracker. Pick out a horse." She chose the light-colored mare. "Good choice. She's large for a Spanish Barb but mellow." They walked the horses over to the barn. Ivy paid close attention while Troy saddled his horse. Then, he pointed to a dark brown saddle in a row of several. "That's the one for your horse."

"I got this," she said with determination.

His prediction was right on. Her tough chic, I-can-do-anything side had reared its foolish head. She struggled with the saddle but managed to carry it over to the horse. Lifting it up and onto the horse's back, which was as high as her head, was another matter. He had to give her credit because she tried. He knew this was an impossible task for a woman her size, so on her third attempt to lift the saddle, he stepped up behind her to lend a hand.

With the saddle in place, she let out a puff of air. "Thanks. That was harder than I thought it would be."

Neither moved. Troy liked her honesty and enjoyed the closeness, and hoped that she did too. He nibbled her sweet-smelling neck before saying softly, "That's a heavy saddle. I've seen wranglers twice your size have trouble with it. You did well."

She made no attempt to move away, so he lingered a while appreciating the contact until the horse snorted and took a step backward. Feeling the saddle on its back, the Barb was anxious to get moving. Troy quickly demonstrated how to tighten the cinch and gave Ivy a boost up.

On horseback, they reached the cow and her calf in just a few minutes. Ivy dismounted right away and the calf bounded over to her. "He looks good. He's going to be fine."

Now, heading west, they rode at a comfortable pace, then turned south on a narrow, unmaintained trail. "I take it this path isn't used by the wranglers or trail riders."

"You're right about that. This portion of the ranch is private."

He knew Ivy spent time wandering around the property, but by the look on her face as they approached the rusty gate, he figured she hadn't been here before. The gate opened allowing them to pass through, then closed.

"How'd you do that?" Ivy asked.

"I have magical powers," he teased, his eyebrows wiggling up and down. "And, I also have a remote that operates the gate."

"You open this rusty old gate with a remote control? Why?"

"The gate just appears to be rusty and old so no one would be tempted to open it. I like modern conveniences, but I also like the look of days gone by around most of the ranch. It's a compromise."

Other than the sound of plodding hooves and the occasional whinny or snort, they rode in silence for another ten minutes or so. When the narrow trail widened and two buildings came into view, strings of fast-moving words tumbled from Ivy's lips.

"What is this place? What goes on here? Why is there such a wide—"

"Whoa! One question at a time, please."

They kept to the edge of the broad, packed dirt trail and rode past the buildings. Troy clued her in about a few things. She didn't need to know everything. This was, indeed, Troy's special place where he operated the breeding portion of the ranch.

"It's magnificent, and so quiet back here."

"That's the way I like it. And, the city-slickers don't need to see horse breeding."

"I want to see everything, and I'd qualify for the city-slicker designation."

"Yeah, but you're different."

"I'm going to take that as a compliment. You still

haven't explained why you need such a wide path here."

"In good time. Come on, follow me. I want to show you my favorite place."

After riding just a few more minutes, they dismounted, walked the horses through a thick stand of pines, and stopped at the base of a waterfall. Troy tied the horses where they could drink from the stream and removed a satchel from one of the saddlebags.

"How would you feel about being late for dinner?"

"Normally, I'd shy away from such a loaded question. But 'late for dinner' is okay with me."

She watched Troy unpack the items in the satchel: two blankets, a small, soft-sided cooler, and a long-nosed lighter. Soon, he'd have a campfire burning, drinks poured, and snacks ready to eat. "After all that transpired yesterday, I felt you deserved another, less eventful picnic."

He spread one blanket for them to sit on and left the other folded. He chuckled subtly watching Ivy's face as she stared at that second blanket. Its only purpose was for warmth, but she didn't know that. Soon, he'd answer the rest of her questions and ask a few of his own.

"Our short ride has become a picnic by a waterfall. I approve. What are we drinking?"

"I'm having a Seven and Seven. I brought Grand Marnier for you. There's sparkling water too."

"How did you know I like Grand Marnier?"

"Let's just say that everywhere I went on my rounds today people were talking about you. Things you did, things you said, things you—"

"Like what?"

"Where should I start? Some folks think you have an unusual love of insects?"

"Now that is ridiculous."

Troy waited patiently for her explanation. When it didn't come, he probed deeper. "What gave people that idea?"

Her lips pouted, her eyes scanned the treetops, and she puffed out an annoyed breath of air. "If you must know, several times today I came across bugs that were trapped inside and were trying to find their way out. I assisted with their exodus. That's all there is to it. No big deal."

Troy found it difficult to hide his smile. "You're a bug saver. That's nice. What about the sandwiches?"

"Oh, that. I mentioned a recipe I'd cooked at work one time. Sort of a Sloppy Joe sandwich. It was loved by all, so I shared it with Kitchi. He had the necessary ingre-dients, so I cooked and served the sandwiches to the ranch guests." She wrinkled her nose and squinted her eyes thinking Troy might be angry about what she'd done. She recalled his words at the cookout. "Guests are not allowed to work here."

"I see. Well, you made Kitchi's day. I've never seen him so happy. And the guests, including myself, thought the sandwiches were great. You're welcome to help Kitchi any time you want to as long as it's okay with him. He usually doesn't want anyone in *his* kitchen, though."

Ivy nodded. "Have you finished giving me the third degree?"

"No, definitely not, but let's take a snack break, relax on the blanket, and enjoy the sound of the falling water for a while." He loved the serenity of this spot, this secluded place he'd visit when he wished to be alone. But this afternoon he wasn't alone. What the heck was he doing?

The sudden, terrified look on Ivy's face changed the direction of his thinking. Her eyes opened wide and her mouth moved, but no sound came out. She pointed behind him, still trying to say something. Troy turned. Not seven yards away, a bear rose up on its hind legs, sniffed the air, and waved its arms. Thankful it was a black bear and not a grizzly, Troy stood and whispered, "Walk slowly to the horses and stay there until the bear moves on."

Luckily, there was no sign of any nearby cubs. The curious bear had stumbled upon them unintentionally and would walk away in a few minutes. If not, Troy would flap that folded blanket around making himself appear large, and then produce a hell of a lot of noise confident that Ivy would join in.

The event played out as he hoped it would, and Ivy was back at his side, her voice operating perfectly. "You have no fear of bears?"

"Not black bears. They are reasonable creatures as long as they don't have cubs with them. I'd have worried had that been a grizzly. They're not as easy to talk to."

"It sounds like you're not afraid of anything."

He thought about his reply. "There are a couple of things." He paused, knowing his answer was both dramatic and humorous. "You... and cats."

"The mountain lion. I forgot about him. It's understandable to fear cats that large. You didn't look afraid, though you did seem on edge."

He let it go for now. Cats were another story for another time. He had one more nagging question to ask, but Ivy spoke up and asked her question first.

"Shouldn't we go? That bear, even if it is a nice bear, could be hiding in the trees watching us. What if it's hungry?"

"We're fine right here." Troy built up the fire, moved the horses closer, and assured her that the bear would keep its distance. He couldn't say the same for himself.

## FOURTEEN

*If only I'd brought my recorder.* That would've made remembering every thought, every sight, every feeling about this beautiful, cozy spot in the woods a whole lot easier. But she hadn't. Her brain would have to do.

The sun dipped below the hills and the temperature dropped quickly. So far, the sweater she wore, the campfire, and the tiny bottles of Grand Marnier were all the warmth she needed.

"Let's see. Back to your questions. You asked one about insects and another concerning sandwiches. Didn't you have a third one?"

"Ah, the perfect segue for my last question, which just happens to be about numbers. So, you're some kind of math geek?"

"Far from it. Math was never my thing."

"Well, the word is out that you're some kind of number, fortune-telling expert. Cody told me that he was a number five; another guest said she was a six, and they learned that from you. Want to enlighten me?"

When she began to shiver, Troy placed the extra blanket around her shoulders. "I'd be happy to. But I am no expert in numerology. It's an interesting hobby for me, that's all, though it's the reason I ended up at this—" She stopped short, not yet ready to admit what had brought her to the ranch in the first place. That might not sit well with Troy.

"Do I have a number?"

"Of course. Everyone does. Your Life Path number is based on your birthday. That's all I figured out for Cody and a few of the guests."

"So, what's my number?"

"What's your birthday?"

"June 26th."

"I also need the year. Won't work without that." He hesitated. Could he have forgotten the year of his birth? *Maybe Troy doesn't want me to know his age.* After a few more sips of his Seven and Seven, he gave her the missing number, though reluctantly.

She calculated quickly, adding the number six (for his month), and the numbers 2+6 = 8 (for the date), and the four numbers representing his year. Then, she reduced all the numbers to a single digit. "Wow!"

"What do you mean, wow?" Troy was curious.

"If I've done this correctly, your Life Path number is Seven. That is so cool."

"Cool how?" he asked, a hint of skepticism in his tone.

Ivy rambled on for a while, excited to be talking about numerology. "I really need my reference book for the details, but number seven is the most magical of all the numbers." That fit, and since he'd just used the word 'magical' when he opened the rusty gate with a remote a while ago, he'd either take his numerology information seriously or tease her incessantly.

"You also possess strength, intelligence, and psychic ability. I think sevens are often loners." She told a little white lie about needing her book. She'd studied all about the number seven before purchasing her plane ticket to Montana.

The gray of dusk had become the dark of night, and the temperature dropped again. Troy joined her under the blanket. "I knew it would be cold tonight. It wasn't my intention to keep you out this long. We'll go as soon as we've warmed up."

"All right. I had a nice time, in spite of the bear." In her way of thinking, he'd saved the best part for last, which was fitting for a seven. Lying wrapped in Troy's arms under the blanket near the campfire was beyond words. But he was a loner according to numerology and her personal observations concurred. Do loners ever partner up for more than a fling? Would such a hot and handsome cowboy accept her, limitations and all?

———

IVY WOKE up early but remained in bed reminiscing and swooning over Troy's passionate goodnight kiss. She snapped her fingers and hummed the old song, *What a Difference a Day Makes*. Wow! Where did that come from?

Admittedly, her time at the ranch resembled a roller-coaster ride complete with highs and lows and everything in between. Never a dull moment. But she had come here following a lead. A lead for a story, a mystery. Now, it seemed there were so many distractions that the mystery was taking a back seat to a relationship that didn't stand a chance.

Still in bed enjoying the cozy warmth, she opened her new journal and read through last night's entry. She read and reread her writing finding it hard to believe those were her words. Her description of the ride, Troy's secret place, and the bear told a tiny but detailed story.

Early yesterday, she'd decided to keep her recorder close by, but her writing would take on a new form. At the end of each day, she'd jot down everything she'd done, noticed, heard, or felt in the spiral notebook she'd labeled, *A Day in the Life of Ivy*.

That recent change in her process had an amazing and almost immediate effect. Freeing her mind from the pressures of writing a novel, ideas and words flowed like never before. True to her own Life Path number, which was the number nine, she'd experienced creative energy vibrating through her fingers, through the pen, and out onto the page last night. If only she could flip a switch and recreate that magical energy for the real story, The Seven Keys Ranch Mystery.

With positive vibes dancing around inside her, she said out loud, "Today will be my lucky day." Could she take advantage of her new found energy and well-stocked river of words? Absolutely! Perhaps she'd stumble upon the information she'd been looking for since arriving at the ranch, or an idea for the perfect ending to her story would pop up giving her words a direction to aim for.

While stretching on the cabin's small front porch, she noticed a note taped to the door. A ranch newsletter? A schedule of activities? Probably, but she was in need of neither. Today she'd explore on her own and bring back the desired facts and new ideas to write about. She grabbed the folded note and went inside to get dressed for the exciting day ahead of her.

With a backpack slung over her shoulder, she headed toward the door. The note still lying on the bed caught her eye, and it seemed to demand her attention. Curiously, she picked it up and began to read. It was from Troy, and it said:

*Hi Ivy,*

*Had to leave before six this morning. I'll be gone all day at a breeders' meeting and then an auction. Would you join me tonight for dinner at my place?*

*Troy*

Taking a pen from her pack, she jotted the words: *I would love to join you for dinner. Call or come by when you're back from your meetings.* She'd leave the note wedged into the jam of his front door after swinging by to see Kitchi and pick up a few snacks for the day's journey.

"Good morning, Ms. Ivy. Going for a hike?"

She had to think about her answer, knowing how close he and Troy were, and the fact that solitary hiking was against the ranch's rules. "Not exactly. But I'm definitely going to walk around some and find inspiration for my writing. I might miss lunch today. Got any snacks I could put in my pack?"

Of course, he did. He let her pick out anything she wanted but gave her that look, the one that let her know he wasn't buying her story. "Stop back when you've had your fill of inspiration."

"Will do." She left with a happy heart knowing this fatherly, Native American man cared about her safety. The feeling was mutual.

After leaving the note for Troy, she stood, then spun full-circle deciding which way to go. She promised herself that she would stick to a visible trail. Getting lost was not part of her plan, but she yearned for a new experience.

Two priorities came to mind—a new experience and safety. She'd search the perimeters of the main ranch property looking for a trail she'd not yet hiked, one without the presence of large, wild animals. She welcomed the company of birds and squirrels, but hoped to avoid a second meeting with a bear or a mountain lion.

She didn't own a gun, but she was not without protection. She had placed fist-sized rocks – like the ones she carried around the ranch to take the place of her daily workouts back home – into her pack. That rock-filled pack would be her weapon, should she need one. She'd also sing as she hiked. Surely, any wild animal would keep its distance from that.

A nameless narrow trail appeared, and off she went. The October air was crisp and cool, nature's soundtrack of birds and squirrels, delightful. With a bounce in her step, she inhaled the fresh air and, for the moment, left thoughts of a romantic relationship and the task of novel writing behind.

The further she walked, the fainter the trail became. At one point, she stopped to examine what appeared to be a fork in the trail. That's when she heard a noise, a rustling sound, then a snap. She held her breath, listened, and looked around to determine the direction the sounds had come from.

"Hello? Is someone there?" The birds and the squirrels were suddenly silent. No one answered her call. *A bear or a mountain lion would not reply. Neither would the Creeping Stick - real or imagined.* Another rustling, another snap. Should she head back? She didn't want to, so she took a few sips of water and listened a while longer.

Convinced the rustling was nothing more than a bird flapping its wings in a bush and the snap possibly a deer stepping on a dried branch, thoughts of hurrying back to the cabin vanished. She could handle a deer she told herself, although her feet had yet to move.

Ivy interpreted the recurrence of birds chirping and squirrels screeching as a positive, all's clear sign, and resumed hiking, though she glanced around and over her shoulder more than before.

By the sun's location, she concluded it must be

midday. Snack time! She left the trail and found a soft, mossy spot beside a tiny stream, a perfect place for note taking about her surroundings, her feelings, and whatever else that came to mind. Thoughts and words, however, came too quickly for her pen to keep up with, so the recorder took over.

What came to mind first was learning about Troy's Life Path number last night. That set her imagination on fire. She pressed the RECORD button.

"It's all coming together in a way I hadn't planned on, but it makes total sense. I'm certain now that Troy was the man in the bar that night talking about the seven keys that kept some kind of money or treasure locked away safely. I knew coming to this ranch was the right thing to do. And now, with so many sevens, there's a story here for sure."

She discovered that she had more questions than answers concerning the connection of the sevens to Troy, but that was okay. Ultimately, the story would be a work of fiction, so accurate facts weren't essential. All she needed were dozens of exciting ideas, mysterious events, and outrageous characters. The thought of filling in all those blanks gave Ivy a thrill. They were out there some-where just waiting to be revealed.

Hearing another unexpected sound, she stopped talk-ing, switched off the recorder, and listened. It sounded like the cry of a tiny baby. Who would be out here with a baby? She didn't think any of the ranch guests had an infant with them. Her mind went in a million directions. More scenarios for a story. Could this be an abandoned infant? When the crying didn't stop, she had to investigate. She'd take a few steps, then pause to listen. She repeated this process, moving closer and closer to the sound. Finally, the source materialized.

## FIFTEEN

The sound hadn't come from a baby but a tiny puppy. What in the world was it doing out here? Had someone dumped an unwanted litter in the woods? Humans have been known for doing worse than that. Maybe they only wanted to get rid of *this* one. She didn't know the answers, and it didn't matter. There was no way she'd leave this tiny creature alone in the woods. She scooped up the puppy into her arms. It wiggled and squirmed its way toward her face, licked her cheek, and nuzzled its scrawny little head under her chin.

Ivy never had a dog of her own, and though it was second nature to her to save any living thing that needed saving, she was surprised how good she felt holding this tiny pup. "I won't let anything hurt you."

She searched the area to be sure there weren't other

pups left alone to die. Between holding the pup and conducting her search, the weight of her pack became too much to deal with. The rocks, her weapons, had to go. Kneeling down, and with mixed feelings, she removed them. The pup crawled into the pack and licked the condensation from her water bottle. *She's thirsty.* Ivy hoped it was beyond the nursing stage because water would have to do for now.

But what would it eat? She examined her snacks: pretzels, an apple, a chocolate breakfast bar, and a few pepperoni sticks. Knowing none of those in their current form were suitable, she took a small bite of the apple, chewed it until it had the consistency of applesauce, then offered it to the pup. No luck. It turned its head away from her offering.

She chewed a pretzel until it became a drippy paste; it received the same disinterested response. There was no way she'd offer it chocolate, but maybe the pepperonis. Putting her teeth and jaw to good use, she managed to soften the tough meat product. The pup took notice and attempted to crawl up Ivy's body to her mouth.

Laughing, delighted to see the tiny dog exhibit some energy, she said, "Okay. Hold your horses, little girl. Your meal is not quite ready for your young tummy." She kept chewing vigorously, then held her breath as she offered the mushy meat to the tiny animal. It seemed to lap at the saliva-coated meat, but it didn't try to chew it. Ivy worried.

There was nothing left to try out there in the forest, so she packed up and trudged back toward the ranch carrying the puppy and singing all the way. Whenever she heard an unidentified sound, she sang louder and walked faster. In the middle of wailing *Life is a Highway*, a brilliant idea came to mind. There was a hotplate in her cabin. She could make a healthy, over-cooked soup that the pup could lap up.

No brilliant ideas presented themselves regarding Troy, however. She'd heard of his dislike for domestic pets – not a single dog or a cat lived at the ranch – and felt certain he wouldn't approve of bringing a puppy home from the forest. That could be a problem... for later.

Right now, the priority was to hide the pup in the cabin's bathroom and snoop around until she found a suitable box that could double as a dog bed for warmth and comfort, and as a crate for keeping her safe. Once she'd accomplished that, she'd find Kitchi and beg for a few appropriate food items. She had it all under control, and as long as she maintained the secrecy of her discovery, her new furry friend, what could possibly go wrong?

"YOUR CARRIAGE AWAITS, MA'AM." Troy laughed when he saw the look on her face.

She looked kind of cute standing there in a long skirt, hands on her hips. "Don't call me ma'am, and I see no carriage. I've heard of a horseless carriage, but never a carriage-less horse."

Ivy was in rare form tonight, and Troy labeled her mood as one with *fun potential*.

"Wait here, I'm going to go change."

"Suit yourself. I think you look mighty fine just the way you are." He watched her open the cabin door just a crack, but then she didn't go in. Instead, she stood there for a few seconds and made loud, throat-clearing noises, and then closed it. Apparently, she'd decided against a wardrobe change. Why? He didn't know. Certain aspects of a woman's reasoning were a mystery to him.

"Okay, so you expect me to get on Tracker with you?"

"That's my plan."

"Maybe I should walk. I don't think your plan is going to work."

"It will." He dismounted, then looked her up and down. "I'll get you on the horse. Just hike that skirt way up."

She gave him a long *you've-got-to-be-kidding* look.

"Time's a wasting. Dinner's getting cold."

The skirt went up, and Troy created a step up with his hands. Ivy now sat on Tracker's back with the entire length of her legs exposed. "I'm not super religious, but I'm going to pray that no one is looking." Troy mounted up behind her, and they rode off at a nice, gentle pace.

The second they stepped into Troy's residence, Ivy said, "Smells delicious. How did you manage to cook a meal when you were gone all day?"

He pointed at the pot on the counter.

"You made a slow-cooker dinner?"

"Yep. Coq Au Vin. Do you have a problem with that?"

"No, I think it's wonderful. I'm surprised, that's all. And, when you left this morning, you didn't know if I'd be able to come over."

"Really? Hmm. I suppose you might have turned me down, but how would your social calendar fill up around here?"

She didn't have an answer. Just as well. The table was set and the food was cooked. All he had to do was pour their drinks, fill their plates, then sit back and enjoy the views – the one out the window and the one across the table. He loved looking at Ivy. He had to admit he was drawn to her natural beauty and her spunky personality, though tonight, something was different. She seemed on edge, anxious, and she fidgeted when he asked about her hike.

"It was nice, very nice. I jotted down some notes, enjoyed nature. Stuff like that."

Not believing the evasive description of her day, he probed deeper. "And I heard you were gone most of the day, even missed lunch."

"The time just flew by," she said, drumming her fingers nervously on the table and taking a big gulp of her drink.

Troy leaned back in his chair, his hand to his chin. "Kitchi mentioned something about soup. He thought you might be cooking some soup in your cabin. Don't we feed you enough?"

"Oh, that. I was in the mood to cook something healthy in case I got hungry later. And, like you said, I missed lunch."

Her story was cute, but too odd to be real. Once again, she was up to something. He changed the subject for now. "Hey, Cody said that he's seen you walking, even running around, long before breakfast is served, carrying a rock in each hand. I didn't believe him, so I thought I'd ask. Do you really do that?"

"Good grief! Are you all spying on me?"

"I don't think so, but I am curious." Seeing her exasperation, he knew that had to be his last prying question of the evening, or the Coq Au Vin might go uneaten.

"Back home, I work out at the gym every day. I want my body to be fit and strong. I'm improvising, doing the best I can. Satisfied?"

"Well, Miss Gym Rat, I'm going to let you in on a little secret. You know that large barn at the far end of the ranch? The one that is always locked?" He knew that she did. She'd snooped around almost every square foot of the main ranch. And now, he had her attention. "Inside that barn is a state-of-the-art gym."

Her eyes opened wide and her jaw dropped in astonishment. "Really? No wonder you're in such great shape."

Keeping in shape was one of his priorities. He was glad that she'd noticed the results of his daily workouts and pleased they'd found some common ground. What delighted him the most, however, was the look on her face when he offered to unlock it for her anytime she desired a workout.

"Even at six in the morning?"

"Yep! But please don't touch the plane, and lock up when you leave. Ready for dessert?" He didn't wait for her answer, but cleared the table of the dinner plates and set down small servings of cheesecake. "I didn't make these. Bought them while I was in town."

She made no comment about the store-bought dessert but gobbled it down in silence. Without a doubt, her mind was not on the food. He could see she was delighted about the existence of a gym, though not sure if she heard him mention his plane. He expected Ivy to question that. A question was never asked, and she resumed her fidgeting.

"How about an after-dinner soak? It will help you relax."

She turned down his offer to immerse herself in his hot, bubbling water saying that she was exhausted from her hike and needed to get some sleep.

"I promise I will be well-rested and energized for your Friday Night Cookout tomorrow." With that, she dashed out the door without another word or even waiting for her carriage-less horse, leaving Troy confused and, once again, wondering what she was up to.

---

IVY WOKE up to the sweet sound of whimpering. It was time to get up. Her puppy needed to go out. At least the tiny dog had slept through the night, something human infants rarely – no, don't go there. She waved that thought away. Literally. She'd let nothing rain on her parade today.

Just watching this adorable creature brought a smile to her face. "Come on, little girl. Let's go." She slipped into her jacket knowing that Montana mornings in October were chilly, and the parade of two stepped onto the porch. Rain. A fine, misty rain greeted them. So much for her previous, positive thoughts. Sighing, she zipped her jacket and scooped up the pup, then hurried to the area behind the cabin. The puppy peed the second Ivy set her down on the damp ground. The rest of their mission took longer. After ten minutes of sniffing everything in sight, the rain-soaked puppy completed its business.

The dampness brought with it a chill even inside the cabin. She turned on the electric heater, then gave the pup and herself a good towel-drying. Now, relatively warm and dry, they were both hungry. Time for soup.

She set the small bowl of puppy soup, yesterday's leftovers, on the floor. Eyeing the speed at which the pup devoured it, she was tempted to dip a spoon into the bowl to taste it before it was gone. Could her concoction be that good? Or was the pup so hungry it would eat anything? She'd never know because before completing her thought the pup had emptied the bowl.

She snuggled with her little fluff-ball on the bed while mentally planning her day. It would consist of: a quick potty walk, a workout in Troy's gym, puppy food preparation, a little writing, and resting. Yes. She'd need time to rest and look great for tonight's cookout.

With all the puppy's needs met, Ivy jogged toward the barn feeling as light as a breeze. No rocks in her hands today. She looked forward to a real workout in a magnificent gym. As she approached her destination, it seemed her gym time might be delayed. Two men wearing tool belts were busy at the gym's door involved in some type of maintenance. Not wanting to interfere with their work, she rearranged the order on her agenda. First, she'd visit the kitchen to gather some ingredients for today's soup making.

"Good morning, Miss Ivy." Kitchi spoke without looking up as he stirred the contents of a pot on the stove.

"That smells good. What is it?"

"Lentil soup. Want some?"

She thought for a moment. Ready-made soup. If the pup liked it, she wouldn't have to cook today. "Can I have a container to go?"

The man shook his head as if annoyed, but Kitchi was rarely displeased. Maybe he'd just wanted a little company while he cooked. She could be that company and return later for soup-making scraps if necessary.

Leaning against the large counter opposite the range, she noticed sweat on Kitchi's brow. His shirt was damp too. The kitchen was cool. Could the man have a fever?

"Are you feeling all right?" She truly was concerned.

"Yes. Why do you ask?"

She thought carefully about the words to use before answering his question. The tactful words didn't come, but a caring tone did. "I thought you might have a fever. You've got some sweat going on there."

That brought a smile to his face. "Been working out. Finished just moments before you entered."

"Really?" Ivy beamed. "You work out in Troy's gym?"

"No."

Did this ranch have two gyms? That would be highly unusual. One gym on a ranch was odd enough. "Then where?"

He looked her straight in the eye, something he rarely did. "In the forest." His one eye refocused on the pot of lentil soup.

*There's a story here, and I'm going to get him to tell it.*

"I'd like to try that. What exactly do you do?"

"I lift logs instead of weights." More soup stirring.

"And...?"

"I do pull-ups using horizontal tree branches."

"What about cardio? That's important too."

"I assure you my heart is well cared for. I walk briskly, I run, I jump over deadfall. Enough?"

This man never ceased to amaze Ivy. "Can I come with you someday? I'd love to try that."

His shaking head declared a definite *no*. "That is my time to commune with nature." He set a container of lentil soup on the counter and nudged it toward her. "Be careful where you wander. I've noticed evidence of a camper or squatter out there."

"Okay." She held up the container. "Thanks. I'm heading back to the gym. The workers should be done by now. See you later."

# SIXTEEN

Ivy looked different tonight, more beautiful than ever with her hair in a loose ponytail and tendrils cascading down. Troy's imagination soared in the form of a mental note: after sufficiently kissing her exposed neck, he'd enjoy letting all of her hair down.

But it was show time now, and he needed to be the ever-charming host of The McAllister Friday Night Cookout. First, however, he'd have a word or two with Ivy, promising to sit by her side tonight even during the entertainment portion of the evening, and maybe steal a kiss.

Troy noticed the odd guest, Lester, wasn't there. What does he do with his time? Not that it mattered. He wasn't actively looking for the petty vandal anymore. Still, he wondered if anyone else had opted out of tonight's event?

The dinner began with lentil soup followed by steak, baked potatoes, and a mixed grill of vegetables. Troy loved this menu but hadn't realized until tonight that it took much longer to serve and eat than when hamburgers were the main dish. All he could think about was spending time with Ivy when the cookout was over. Patience eluded him.

After several sing-along songs and one duet sung by Saige and Willy, Troy asked, "Hey, Cody, could you lead us in *The Bear Went Over the Mountain*?" He had a plan. Tonight's story would be about a bear. He could tell by the look on Ivy's face as he began that she understood that certain elements of their picnic would be part of his story.

The festivities were still in full swing after Troy told his tale. Guests danced to the music and roasted marshmallows over the fire. Troy whispered something to Kitchi, then took Ivy's hand and they dashed in the darkness to his private barn where nothing would disturb them. Tonight was the night, and they both knew it. One serious romp in the hay coming up.

---

IVY WATCHED as Troy unlocked the barn's door and flipped a switch that turned on a row of bright track lights, which he quickly dimmed. She'd avoided the gym that morning due to the presence of the workers. Later, she was too busy with her puppy to take advantage of Troy's recent offer. Seeing it for the first time, she was awestruck.

"Wow! You really do have a state-of-the-art gym set up here." He also hadn't been kidding about the airplane. There it was. *The owner of the ranch must be richer than rich to have all this cool stuff. No wonder he kept the door locked, and spent so much time at the ranch.*

"Come on, let's go to the loft. You can work out with this equipment tomorrow. Tonight, you're working out with me." He pointed to the ladder and motioned for her to go first. He followed close behind, his hands on her waist.

Ivy didn't dare look down as she made the vertical climb upward, and she wondered which took her breath away more: the height and the steepness, or the hot, sexy man mere inches away. Heights had bothered her – creating a feeling of falling in her belly – ever since she was nine years old and had witnessed her brother's glider accident. Seeing him drop from the sky and unable to help him, left her with an emotional scar and an inner need to help others. Making love to a man capable of stealing her heart brought on a different set of emotions.

*Stop thinking! Live in the present.*

After reaching the top of the ladder and moving away from the loft's edge, she smiled. "A hayloft without hay. I think I like that. But where do we sit? I see no furniture."

His eyes twinkled and his teeth sparkled even in the delicate light. He pressed a button on the wall with the drama of a magician. The wall moved to the side revealing a rustic-looking bedroom. He shrugged. "This is my hideaway. Sometimes I need to get away from it all. Get back to my roots." Then he put a finger to his lip and added, "You and Kitchi are the only ones who know about this. And it needs to stay that way. Okay?"

Ivy nodded, blown away once again. This man was full of surprises. "I want to know more about you, Troy," she said as she unbuttoned and removed her shirt exposing a silky, white cami. "About your family, your past, your fears. Something other than what I can see."

She knew that face. His thinking face, but with a subtle grin. "Right now, I can see that you're chilled," he said. "And I can fix that." He removed his hat, his shirt, and his boots and led her to the bed. "I'll tell you a story that I've never told before, but first I want to hold you in my arms, skin-on-skin, and let our bodies take charge."

They'd been shirtless during the cow/calf incident, and naked during their last spa encounter, but tonight was different. The stakes higher, her breath shorter. Troy's sweet and gentle side had surfaced. Her head rested on his shoulder as he stroked her hair, her face, even her ears. She could get used to this.

"Troy?"

"Yeah?"

"I've felt relaxed and wonderful the past few days partly because nothing odd has occurred. No vandalism of any kind. I have a hunch the culprit got bored and went away."

"If he's smart, he did. If there is a next time, I'm not about to let it go. I will track him down. But tonight is ours, no one else's. I'm falling for you, Ivy, and I don't know what to do about that."

Ivy's Life Path number was nine, and many of a nine's characteristics served her well. Some, however, were problematic and soon to rear their ugly heads. For now, she listened to his words. She'd fallen for him days ago... and didn't know how to handle that. What could either of them do? She'd be going back to Denver in less than a week. It would be time to end their budding relationship, to let it go before it had truly begun.

"You can tell me to back off any time, Ivy. I'll understand. I've never bothered with a real relationship, except for the one with Tracker. I have no expertise in this area."

She nodded. "That makes two of us on this blind-leading-the-blind road to nowhere."

"What I do best is run this ranch."

"It's an amazing ranch. The owner must be pleased."

Suddenly, his face wore a look she'd never seen before. "Yeah, about that—"

Not wanting to hear details concerning the business or the owners of the ranch during this special time with Troy, she interrupted saying, "Shut up and kiss me."

"Yes, ma'am." Troy seemed more than happy to oblige. He began with a long, deep sensual kiss on her lips, then moved his mouth lower. She shivered when he kissed her neck.

"I think this might be a good time for that story." Her words trailed out in a breathless whisper.

Frowning, he hesitated. To be helpful, she nudged him a little. "Was it a family story you'd wanted to tell?" He shook his head. Apparently, he'd changed his mind about telling her a story tonight, or maybe it had more to do with the timing of her request.

"All right. Then tell me about one of your fears." To break the ice, she offered to go first. "I'm not good with heights. Just climbing up the ladder was tough and made me feel dizzy. Climbing down will be a bigger challenge. Your turn."

"I'm sorry, Ivy. I had no idea of your difficulty with heights. I do understand fear, and I wouldn't have brought you up here had I known."

"It's okay. I can handle it. What fear are you dealing

with?" Would he be willing to show her he had a vulnerable side? She had doubts about that.

"Cats."

"Cats?" Was he kidding? She recalled he'd mentioned something about cats before. Still, she smothered the urge to giggle.

"Yes. I have a fear of cats. Before I go any further, you must swear never to repeat what you are about to hear."

She raised her hand. "I swear I'll never tell. Cross my heart and hope to die."

He propped his head up with his arm and began. "When I was seven or eight years old, I tried to teach myself to drive one of my dad's ATVs. It didn't go well. I couldn't reach the pedals or see over the steering wheel, but I was determined to do it."

He paused and blew out a long breath. This amazing man seemed uncomfortable telling a story about a cat. "I ran over and killed my favorite cat. I cried hard that day and many days after that. I never forgave myself. My sadness turned into a fear of cats. I admit that is a strange outcome, but it was because of that cat that I felt so damn awful for so long. I had no tolerance for feeling bad back then, or even today, for that matter."

"Wow, that's some story. I'm so sorry. Are you still sad about the cat?"

"No, not really. But I'll never have another pet. I couldn't go through that again. After all this time, I still haven't been able to shake my unreasonable reaction to cats." He got up and walked to the corner of the loft, returning with a small bottle of sparkling water in each hand.

Ivy thought about the puppy and was thankful it wasn't a cat, though it did fall into the 'pet' category. She'd try never to use the phrase *it's raining cats and dogs* in his presence and she doubted he'd tolerate her pup. She also regretted asking him to tell about one of his fears. Had she ruined this special night for them? Probably. She reached for her clothes, but Troy stopped her. "I'm okay, really. And, like I said earlier, this is our night."

The romantic moment returned and the caressing recommenced, but this time with a new sense of urgency. They desperately needed the closeness, the release, and each other. Ivy had never been so hot, so ready, in her entire life. Troy reached under his pillow and took out a condom. He was ready and prepared to make love.

"We don't need that," she whispered, hoping he'd enjoy the intensified sensation and the closeness without the latex barrier between them. Instead, he glared at her, stood, and quickly dressed. Her comment had struck a nerve, an icy-hot nerve. But why? Confusion clouded her thinking. "What's the matter? I was trying to—"

"Stop! I've heard those words many times before. I'm not falling for it, Ivy, not even with you." At the top of the ladder, he turned and added, "There's only one reason a woman declines a condom."

The hollow sound of his boots stomping down the ladder echoed in her ears. He'd left her lying high up in the loft, alone. She knew he was gone when the barn door slammed shut. A cold shiver traveled up her spine and her eyes overflowed with tears. Shoulders shaking, she sobbed like never before. "You're wrong, Troy. There's another reason." Her loaded words arrived too late and were heard by no one.

Had she misjudged him, or was this some kind of payback from the universe for withholding the truth? She lay curled up in the bed overcome with sadness and hoping he'd return. If only she could explain the comment that had brought on such a feeling of rage within the man she cared for. Surely, he would have a change of heart or at least know she had no intention of trapping him.

Ivy drifted in and out of sleep when something prompted her eyes to open. A sound? The darkness? The lights no longer illuminated the barn. Either they'd been on a timer, or someone had been here and turned them off.

She longed to be in her cabin with the little pup that would greet her with enthusiasm, give her kisses, and love each and every word she spoke. There was no way she would climb down the steep ladder in total darkness unable to see her own hand in front of her face. She curled up again and waited for the morning light to show her the way.

ANGRY WITH HIMSELF, Troy stomped the ground, kicking rocks and cursing at the world. How could he have been so naïve, so damn stupid? She was just like all the other women, maybe worse. Ivy was a thief. She'd stolen his heart and set the perfect trap. But it wouldn't work. He'd learned a valuable lesson tonight.

With no desire to talk with Cody or Kitchi, he skirted the cookout area hoping to make it home without being seen. The guests had already left, but his two main men were still packing up. They knew him a little too well. They'd assume something had gone wrong in paradise and take great pleasure in teasing him about it. No, he wasn't up to that. So he walked quickly and quietly toward his residence. What would he do when he got there? He hadn't a clue. This was one of those rare times he craved a real alcoholic drink.

Could he make do with his unique version of a Seven and Seven? Or a flute of fake champagne? Or a wine glass of fictitious pinot noir? He'd ignore the craving. Sparkling water right out of the bottle would be his choice. With no one else around, there was no need to appear cool or hip and pretend to imbibe alcohol. Still, deep down, he wanted to wash away the bad feelings caused by thoughts of Ivy.

The slight pressure of slipping the key into the lock made the door open even before he'd had a chance to turn the key. He cussed at the notion of not closing his door firmly when he'd left earlier. Could this day get any worse? A quick soak in the spa and he'd hit the hay. Tomorrow, he'd start fresh.

He didn't bother with the entryway light or even the living room light. Instead, he headed straight for his bedroom in the dark. "Ow!" He tripped and nearly fell, then reached for the closest light switch to get a visual on the item that had almost brought him down. *What the hell?*

He ran from room to room turning on every light in his home. His place had been vandalized. Trashed. Every piece of wall décor was either crooked or on the floor. Every drawer opened and some emptied. Furniture was pulled away from the walls. Even the fridge and the freezer had been ransacked.

He searched for his walkie-talkie, that being the only way to communicate with Kitchi and Cody if they were still at the cookout area. He couldn't find it in the mess. It wasn't anywhere near its usual location. His handgun was missing too. Troy took off running to inform his men.

"Guys. We've got a problem. Saddle up four horses and bring them and whoever is sleeping in the bunkhouse over to my office." They tipped their hats. Cody dashed toward the horse barn, Kitchi to the bunkhouse. Troy headed to his office hoping to find his other guns right where they should be.

Troy paced as he spoke to his men. "My personal residence was vandalized sometime during the cookout. Everything inside was scattered or broken. Someone is searching for something and they're determined to find it, though I have no idea what... or why.

We all need to be on high alert and armed. You all know how to use a gun, right?" There were nodding heads all around. "Good. Keep in mind the guns are only for your protection. We want to apprehend, not kill. We're going to work in teams of two, on four-hour shifts. Cody, I need you put a schedule together."

They spent another hour working out the details and finalizing their strategies. The culprit would be identified and removed within twenty-four hours. That was the plan. Not knowing who that was – a guest or a stranger – added to their challenge. It also added to their excitement. Nothing like this had ever happened at the ranch before. Welcome to the Wild West.

Troy shoved a pistol into his shoulder holster and put on a denim jacket to keep the gun out of sight. He didn't want to alarm his guests with the sudden appearance of a weapon. He'd be on duty twenty-four seven. He wasn't scared, but he was mad as hell. Solving this mystery, taking down the vandal, might award him hero status – something he'd always longed for. *Bring it on!*

# SEVENTEEN

The moment she'd anxiously waited for had arrived. The lightless barn turned to dark gray, exposing the outline of its contents. Sitting where the ladder met the surface of the loft, Ivy peaked over the edge to determine its sturdiness. Even with Troy right behind her, last night's steep ascent had blurred her vision and taken her breath away. This morning she'd be on her own.

The situation was better than she'd hoped for. The ladder, her only way down to the ground, was firmly attached to the loft and wasn't going to tip over. The steps were flat, narrow boards, better than the rungs of a typical ladder. Twinges of confidence jiggled around in her belly. She could do this. She had to do this. The puppy had been alone for hours, too many hours.

After giving some thought to her physical position during the descent, she chose to face the ladder. Though she'd need to use caution as she placed each foot on the next narrow, unseen board, she'd have a better grip on the ladder's sides. She'd reach the floor without needing to look down.

Once both feet were on solid ground, her usual level of confidence reappeared. Her main mission? Return to her puppy with something yummy for it to eat. Her puppy soup had worked well yesterday using just a few breakfast and lunch scraps, but she needed to make more. First stop, the kitchen.

She gently closed the barn's door not wanting to disrupt the profound stillness of the early hour or call attention to herself, then walked quickly toward the kitchen's back entrance wondering if Kitchi might already be there. Did she want to see him? Could she trust him with the knowledge of her new four-legged roommate? He did seem to be Troy's closest... employee, friend, all of the above. She couldn't define their relationship. Whatever it was, he might feel an obligation to share that information.

The dark sky became a lighter shade of gray. Her surroundings, monochromatic. Glancing from left to right, she felt as if she were watching an old western movie shot in black and white. She saw no light shining through the kitchen windows and had mixed feelings about being the first to arrive. No Kitchi, no explaining to do, but the door was likely locked.

To her surprise, the door was not only unlocked, but it was also slightly ajar. She tiptoed in and went right to the huge refrigerator hoping to find a few leftovers from the cookout. She wouldn't take much, just what she could hold in her hand. Without any type of cooler or small fridge in the cabin, she'd only make one day's worth of puppy food at a time.

Startled by a sound coming from the opposite end of the kitchen, she looked up expecting to see a critter that might have entered the same way she had. Instead, what she saw looked like a shadow darting quickly from the room.

"Kitchi? Is that you?" No answer. She grabbed a frozen hamburger, a hot dog, and a few carrot sticks. Looking over her shoulder, she dashed for the door and collided with Kitchi.

"Miss Ivy, you're up early." He looked at the odd variety of food items in her hand. "Hungry?" he asked, a perplexed look on his face.

"I couldn't sleep so I was walking around. Thought I'd say hello if you were here."

"Well, here I am. We can talk while I make breakfast for the guests."

There was no time for talking. A hungry, lonely puppy was waiting and likely needed to take a trip outside if it wasn't already too late.

"What is the real reason for your visit?"

This man could not be fooled, but she'd try. "I've taken on a new hobby. Soup-making. I might even write a book, a cookbook. Yeah. I'll call it *The Soup Cabin*." Proud of her imaginative, on the spot answer – a lie, really – she hurried toward the door needing to get to her cabin, to the puppy. "I almost forgot. When I arrived, the door wasn't locked. It wasn't even closed. Then I thought I saw someone over by the stoves. Weird, huh?"

"Go home, Miss Ivy. And stop walking around in the dark by yourself."

———

CLEANING up the place wasn't high on his list, but if he looked at it, the mess bothered him greatly and he did want to locate his cell phone. Fortunately, it rang and he followed the sound. No one ever called him at five in the morning, but all things considered, he felt a flash of concern. It had to be a wrong number, bad news, or – someone had cornered their vandal.

"Troy here."

"Come on over, boss. I'll make you breakfast. We've got something to talk about."

Still wearing yesterday's clothing, he pulled on his boots and rode the quad to the kitchen. "So talk."

Kitchi set a cup of strong coffee in front of Troy. "When I arrived, just before 5:00 a.m., Ivy was leaving with a few items of food in her hand. Said she was making soup. You'd think she was feeding the homeless."

Troy shook his head and shrugged his shoulders. "That is something she might do."

"Yeah, but not at the ranch. She's been acting strange the past twenty-four hours. Haven't you noticed?"

"Did you call me over here to tell me Ivy is making soup?"

"No, but I do think you should ask her who was at the cookout last night. Better yet, ask who was *not* there. She's become acquainted with most of the guests. She'll know."

"You ask her. We're not on speaking terms right now."

Giving Troy an emotionless stare, Kitchi said, "Okay, but there's one more thing. Miss Ivy said the door was open when she arrived and she thought she saw someone in here. The lock had been tampered with. I checked."

Frustrated, Troy nodded. "I'll spread the word."

TIRED of calling her new furry friend Puppy, one of Ivy's goals for the day was to come up with a perfect name for her. She multi-tasked, watching the playful pup, thinking of names, and stirring the soup wishing she had a microwave. It was taking far too long to turn the food on hand into a soft meal suitable for a dog this young.

"Let's sneak out for a real walk while your food cools." She constructed a makeshift harness from an old piece of rope and attached it to one of her belts. It wasn't pretty, but it was practical.

Her cabin's location – the furthest one from the ranch's other cabins and buildings and set twenty feet from the tree line – was a stroke of luck. Once in the trees, they'd be hidden from curious eyes. Ranch guests would love to see the pup, but she couldn't risk it, at least not yet. Troy, Kitchi, and Cody would not share their enthusiasm. She'd bet money on that.

With her journal, a water bottle, a snack-pack of applesauce, and the last pepperoni stick, Ivy and the nameless pup ventured out to find a cozy spot for some safe, outdoor fun. Only one day after its rescue, the tiny dog's energy had increased by leaps and bounds. Today, she hopped and turned in circles attempting to catch her tail. For her next trick, she bit and shook the belt-leash.

The pup's delight was contagious. Ivy had never felt happier, and words describing this blissful feeling flowed from her pen like a catchy tune dancing from the flute of a wood nymph.

She glanced up when the pup's movement ceased. Focused, it crouched, seriously stalking a bug. This, too, was adorable until she pounced on and ate it. "No!" Horrified, Ivy scooped her up and proceeded to pry the insect from her tiny, sharp-toothed mouth. "Ow!" she exclaimed, and managed to pull out what was left of the fuzzy creature. "You must be really hungry to eat *that*. Here, try this." She placed a gumball size dollop of apple-sauce on the palm of her hand. The pup gobbled it down proving that store-bought applesauce tasted better than a masticated bite of a real apple.

Playtime had become naptime. After a few sweet moments of snuggling in Ivy's arms, she wobbled over to a nearby pine sapling, curled up under it, and fell asleep. Ivy wrote while the pup rested.

*A night filled with hope, yes, that's what it was. The woman walked toward the cave with confidence. What would she find? She didn't know yet. But she would find something. Something that would uncover the mystery of the keys...*

Proud of her four-page accomplishment and ready to head back to the cabin, her focus returned to the pup. But the pup was gone. No! That can't be. She must be looking toward the wrong tree. She saw no evidence of the adorable fluff-ball sleeping peacefully under any nearby pine tree. She rushed closer to the spot where the pup should have been, but all she found was the belt-leash with one end severely chewed. Panic set in. No way could her tiny dog survive on its own. How could she have let this happen?

A search began. Not wanting to frighten the young dog and cause it to run further away, she stepped lightly, slowly, and called out softly, "Hey, little girl, let's go home. Come on." She circled their cozy spot many times increasing the circumference with each pass. Unable to find the tiny dog, she took out the remaining portion of applesauce hoping to entice the pup to find her, and kept circling. *Maybe I should name her Houdi-ni.*

"Looking for this?"

Startled, Ivy turned and saw Kitchi holding her puppy. "What are you doing out here?" She reached for the tiny dog.

"I might ask you the same, but I have a more pressing question. What are you doing with a coyote pup?"

Her eyes widened and her lips parted in astonishment. "A coyote?"

"Yes. It is shocking. It's too late in the year for coyote

pups to be out and about. I will deal with that part of this phenomenon later."

She asked again, "What brings you out here today?" Holding the wiggling pup, she sat on the ground. Kitchi followed suit.

"I believe you know that the forest is my gym, and I like to walk where others do not. I assure you, it was never my intention to find you here with a coyote pup. I did notice our skinny guest, Lester. He did not strike me as a forest walker, and I felt he was up to something. I followed, but when he saw me, he turned and hurried back toward the ranch. That's when this little gal poked her head out from the shadows of some bushes back there and yipped. And here we are."

Ivy held up the pup with both hands so they were nose to nose. "Shadow. I'm going to call you Shadow. That's a perfect, natural name for you." Shadow showered her with coyote kisses. Likely a rare phenomenon for humans.

"You do know a pup this young, even if she could be reunited with her pack, would not survive a Montana winter."

"I figured she was in danger regardless of her heritage. That's why I brought her home with me. Didn't know she was a coyote."

Shadow seemed overjoyed with the attention of two

people, jumping from one lap to the other. They spent the next half hour discussing the pup's future. They reached no viable conclusions, but during their time in the forest together, Ivy felt a new closeness to the man and considered asking about his eye patch. When he handed her the pup and stood to leave, she asked, "Why do you wear that patch over your eye?"

He sat back down. "You are the first person to ask me that question."

His statement added to her curiosity. Did no one else ask because asking was inappropriate or rude? Were they afraid he'd be angry? Were they waiting for him to bring up the subject? She looked at him with a questioning expression knowing it was too late to take back her words.

The silence combined with his penetrating, one-eyed stare was unbearable. She wanted to flee the awkward situation she'd created, and would have, but he continued to speak.

"I was told my mother dropped me when I was an infant, and the fall damaged my eye beyond repair. I have no memory of the incident, so don't expect details."

"She must have felt terrible to have hurt her own baby."

"I don't know. My father sent her away and she never came back. When I was older, in my heart I forgave her, but she'll never know that. I think she never forgave herself."

"How awful. I'm so sorry that happened. I wish—"

"What's done is done. Not everyone is cut out to be a mother."

*Am I one of those women?*

The Native American man vowed to keep her secret and supply proper food for the tiny coyote. He also handed out some fatherly advice. "Remain close to your cabin when taking Shadow outside. Stay in plain sight when walking anywhere alone."

Kitchi left running. Lunchtime was fast approaching. Watching him go, she held the tiny pup close to her heart and struggled with the sudden onset of emotion that swirled inside her. Ivy knew him to be incredibly intuitive. What did he know? His words sent a chilly wave of apprehension through her entire body. As tears rolled down her cheeks, she wondered who those tears were for.

## EIGHTEEN

Before she'd finished her lunch, Kitchi set a package wrapped in foil by her plate, then gave her a wink. Ivy knew it was food for Shadow. A few of the guests, the ones with raised eyebrows, viewed the individual attention as a reason for rumors.

"Looks like you've got a friend in the kitchen," teased one of them.

Ivy shrugged feigning ignorance of the cook's action.

"I think he's a bit old for you, dear."

The guests adored Ivy and took great pleasure in joking with her. Everyone added his or her two cents. Everyone except Lester, who kept his head down and his mouth full. He was also the first to leave the table. Why was he even there? He never interacted with anyone, never even rode a horse. Apparently, he did wander in the forest. Such an odd guy.

Ivy was next to leave, anxious to return to her cabin, see her coyote pup – she loved how exotic that sounded – and continue where she'd left off with her writing. Now that she'd convinced herself that jotting down thoughts in her journal was the way to go, words and story snippets flowed.

It occurred to her that she hadn't been snooping around the ranch lately in search of the story details she'd expected to find there. She didn't need Troy or his story anymore, though the fascinating words she'd overheard in the Denver bar were never far from her thoughts. No, she would generate plenty of her own ideas.

Walking down the dimly lit hallway that connected the dining room to The Lodge, she stopped suddenly at the sound of a heated conversation. Not wanting to intrude, she took a few steps backward, but after hearing the word *treasure* curiosity got the better of her. She inched silently forward, closer to the voice.

There stood Lester with his back to her, a phone pushed against his ear. "I'm sorry Mr. V. I'm doing the best I can... I've looked everywhere... Just that one safe is all I found... No! Don't hurt her. She's young and innocent." He seemed to be listening to a lengthy monologue, as he said nothing for a quite a while, but wiped the sweat from his brow with the sleeve of his shirt.

Lester's voice had dwindled to nothing more than a pitiful squeaking sound. "I can't do it. That's not part of our deal." He said nothing more, but listened and sobbed until he placed the phone into his pocket and shuffled out.

Ivy wanted to rush after him, help him. The man definitely needed a friend. Selfishly, she thought Lester must have one heck of a story to tell. It could be a win-win situation. She dashed out the door, but he was nowhere in sight. Perhaps fate had intervened.

If a guest were in trouble, Troy would want to know. In spite of last night's disaster, she returned to The Lodge and knocked on the door to his office. Then she pounded, but there was no answer. From there, she headed for his personal residence only to meet with the same result. Two options remained, the breeding area and the stables.

She found Cody at the stables and asked him if he'd seen Troy. His response came as a surprise. "I can't help you, Miss Ivy," he said, his voice totally devoid of expression. The man hadn't even looked up but kept brushing the horse standing next to him.

Fate had intervened again. Just as well. Troy hadn't spoken to her since last night in the loft when he'd jumped to conclusions – mistaken assumptions – and wouldn't give her time to explain. Thinking back to that awful situation, she wondered if she would have revealed her reason for not needing him to use a condom. Honestly, she wasn't sure.

Ivy jotted down a short note that read: *I need to see you ASAP*. She folded it, wrote 'Troy' on it, and left it in Kitchi's kitchen. He'd likely be the first one to see the absent cowboy. She walked back to her cabin reevaluating all the events of the past week.

Her short walk was fruitful and her decisions took a new direction. Keeping her distance from Troy received top billing on her To Do list. She didn't need a self-centered, ego-driven cowboy in her life. Her days of trying to fix problems around the ranch were over, and she'd bury any remaining inclinations to treasure hunt for the purpose of finding a story to write. She'd spend the rest of her ranch days drafting a story of her own and enjoying Shadow. Even so, her upcoming departure dominated her thoughts.

---

TROY, needing a distraction, rode Tracker over to the arena to watch the horse ladies practice their routines. He could count on their reaction to his presence. Nothing ever changed: the waving hands, the smiling red lips, and the jiggling, perky breasts. They treated him like a prince. Yeah, he could count on all that.

He lapped up the attention for a while. It was good for his ego. They teased, they flirted, and posed plenty of offers he might have taken in the past. Today, however, those offers left him empty, and eventually, he found the whole scene annoying. Every one of those women knew he owned the ranch; they wanted his money and the status being his woman would bring.

Troy wanted Ivy, a natural beauty who asked for nothing. It was as simple as that. She still had no idea that he owned The Lonely Horse Ranch. She was interested in him thinking he was merely a ranch manager. He shook his head, knowing he'd made too many mistakes and doubted she'd ever speak to him again.

He thought about hitting the gym, pumping some iron, but didn't have the energy. After riding Tracker in pointless circles, Troy took an unscheduled trip to town to pick up items he did not need. He ate junk food – greasy fried chicken and an ice cream cone – before heading home.

Upon his return, Troy found Cody pacing outside the door to his office. The cowboy looked frustrated as he greeted his boss. He wanted permission to call a meeting with the wranglers. Ordinarily, he wouldn't need permission to do this but thought an update regarding their unofficial detective duties was in order.

"Can I ask them to meet us here right away?" Cody's serious tone was overtaken by a chuckle and a smirk. "Seems you might have pressing plans for—" He stopped mid-sentence and pointed to the items in Troy's hands.

"Huh?" Troy looked down at the Cowboys & Indians Magazine he held in one hand and the toy horse that resembled Tracker in the other. Embarrassed he said, "Call the damn meeting."

They gathered in the dining room where Kitchi had set out plates of brownies left over from dinner. Since they'd begun taking four-hour shifts in pairs there'd been little to report. To the best of their knowledge, nothing out of the ordinary had happened.

"That's right, and after those two undercover guys arrived, it's been quiet, no additional vandalism. Nothing." The wranglers all shook their heads in agreement, feeling good about the situation.

Troy, on the other hand, was baffled. "What are you talking about?"

Cody looked at Troy and shrugged. This was news to him too.

"The two guys in denim overalls looking like repairmen," Willy added. "They got tool belts and everything. Man, that was a brilliant idea. You hired them, right?"

"No, I did not! I would have told you if I'd hired any outsiders. When and where did you see them?"

The wranglers couldn't get the details of their stories straight and began to argue. They'd mistakenly assumed the guys in denim were helping out and hadn't paid close enough attention. Even if they weren't the vandals, they were trespassing and, presumably, up to no good.

Troy spoke words he'd never said before. "Cancel all of tomorrow's rides." The wranglers' eyes widened. "There aren't many guests here now, anyway. It's all hands on deck tonight and tomorrow. Search the place. Call me immediately if anything looks suspicious. We will find and apprehend these denim delinquents within twenty-four hours."

FUR TICKLED HER NOSE. Ivy gently brushed at the odd feeling until a tiny tongue licked the corner of her mouth. "Stop that," she mumbled, not yet in touch with the real, wide-awake world. It was the faint attempt at howling just inches from her ear that got her full attention.

She laughed. "Shadow, I forgot you were in bed with me. What're you're doing up before the sun?" She'd also forgotten to flip the heat on before falling asleep. The cabin was so cold she could see her breath. Motivated, she jumped up, turned on the heat, and dressed in a pair of cargo pants and a long-sleeve t-shirt, topped with her thickest sweatshirt – a Denver Broncos hoodie.

Out of the blue, she began to sing *Me and my Shadow.* She had no idea how such an old song emerged from her brain, nor could she remember the rest of the words, but had a sudden urge to tap dance, and so she did. Shadow pranced around her feet, then ran to the door and peed right there. A decent approximation, she thought. Laughing again, Ivy scooped up the pup and dashed behind the cabin. There, Shadow finished what she'd started. "Good girl."

The pup loved Kitchi's concoctions. She gobbled down the food and licked the bowl clean every time. She'd make one more trip out back with the pup – cautiously, Ivy looked both ways as if crossing a busy street – for a quick romp and fresh air, before jogging over to the gym.

Did she hope to run into Troy? Of course not. *Good grief. I'm lying to myself.* But she wondered if the gym door would be unlocked, or if he had reneged on his offer. Maybe those repairmen were changing the lock. Ugh! Time would soon tell.

The ranch was eerily quiet except for the gentle whinnies and occasional nickering from the horses and chirping from a few early birds. But the sky was still too dark and the hour too early for most of the guests. They'd only begin to stir when it was time for breakfast.

"Son-of-a-gun!" She spoke with glee in her voice. "He'd opened the gym for me." With the palm of her hand, she felt the inside wall near the door for the light switch. "Ow!" What she found was rough wood and now had a splinter the size of a toothpick stuck in her hand. "Damn."

"Miss Ivy, help! Please help," a weak, male voice called out from within the barn. She could barely see the outline of a thin figure dragging his leg and approaching the open door. Instinctively, she ran to meet the person in need and helped him sit down, then returned to the wall determined to find a light source.

"Voila! Let there be—"

From behind, a hand covered her mouth and nose with a moist cloth. She gasped for air and tried to pry the fingers from her face, but her head suddenly felt light and her body woozy. That's when she noticed the odor, a smell she was familiar with. Was it Ether? What the hell?

Suddenly, her knees buckled as she fell to the floor, and a foul-tasting liquid filled her mouth. She was too weak and dizzy to spit or cough and felt as if she were drowning. Then came an odd tugging sensation. Someone was dragging her across the floor by her feet. "You're the… you're… the…" she managed to mumble just before something hard and heavy collided with her head.

Pain. So much pain.

Then nothing.

Darkness.

## NINETEEN

"Morning, Kitchi. Something sure smells good." Without a word, the cook poured coffee with one hand, pulled a folded-up piece of paper from his pocket with the other, and handed them to Troy.

"That hits the spot," he said, taking a sip and opening the note. "Hmm. It's from Ivy and she wants to see me ASAP. When did she give you this note?"

"She didn't. I found it on the counter this morning. My guess? She left it here sometime yesterday, but I just now noticed it."

"When was the last time you saw her?" His gut told him there was a problem.

"Yesterday at lunch."

His gut screamed now, and he did not like the way that felt. "Did she seem all right then?"

Kitchi nodded. Troy had known this man for years. He was a man who spoke the truth, but that was not the case today. "Well?"

"She might have been distracted. She seemed busy, in a hurry."

Troy stomped out leaving his full coffee cup on the stainless steel counter. Next stop, his office. Maybe she'd left another note with more information. Or perhaps he was making a big deal out of nothing. Either way, he needed to know.

He found no helpful information but paced back and forth thinking about what he'd done and hadn't done in the loft Friday night. Ivy had turned his world upside down, shaken his belief in his own past choices, and unwittingly coaxed him from his comfort zone.

Yesterday, away from the ranch, he'd done some soul searching for the first time in his life. She wasn't his type, but he wanted her. *Annoying* was her middle name, but he missed her. They hadn't yet made love, but he loved her. Yes, as strange and shocking as that seemed, he loved her.

What had her note said? She needed to see him ASAP? And no one has seen her since yesterday's lunch?

Several scenarios galloped through his head. More vandalism? A guest's comment she thought he should know about? A needed repair? A mountain lion sighting? Something was wrong, he felt it. Did she want to leave the ranch? *I couldn't blame her if she did.* Now he needed to see *her* ASAP.

He headed over to the stables where the trail horses were housed. Cody had ten horses tied to the hitching post and saddled up ready for the morning riders. "No rides today, remember?"

"Yes, boss. I thought I'd pretend today was just a regular day so our culprits wouldn't catch on to our plan."

"Good thinking. Have you seen Ivy?"

"Nope. Saw her yesterday. She was looking for you."

"What did you tell her?"

"Nothin'. I hadn't seen you." Cody's voice carried a tone of annoyance. "Didn't know where you were for a while. Nobody did."

Troy stared at his head wrangler, adjusted his hat, and continued his search. He'd check with Saige, then head over to Ivy's cabin. He should have gone their first but wasn't quite ready to discover that she might have left the ranch. He looked in all directions as he walked hoping to see her jog by. She ran every day.

Far off in the distance, he thought he saw the barn's

door ajar, the barn that housed the gym and his plane, but he needed to get closer to be sure. Then, a hopeful thought came to mind. Of course, Ivy was there working out. Somewhat relieved, he strode in that direction.

"Hey, babe. Kitchi just gave me your note," he called out as he stepped inside. Instead of Ivy, there stood one of the rarely seen guests, Lester. "Sorry, this area is off limits. You need to leave. Go grab some breakfast."

"Oh, I'll be on my way, no doubt about that, and so will you."

The wimpy-looking intruder stood his ground. What the hell?

"Miss Ivy is in trouble. We've got to save her, and I know where she is."

This man's words were borderline crazy, but he'd been odd from day one. Troy played along for a few minutes, wishing he had his walkie-talkie with him. He'd have called for a couple of wranglers to escort this guy from the property.

"Okay, if you know so damn much, tell me where she is."

"Can't do that, but we can get there in time to save her if we use your plane."

The guy was out of his ever lovin' mind. Troy could humor him no longer. "You want me to believe she's wandered off so far that we need a plane to get to her? I've heard enough. Get the hell out of here before I have you thrown out."

"I'm a paying guest. You can't throw me out."

"Watch me." It occurred to Troy that no one had seen Ivy since midday yesterday. Could she have wondered that far? Did she need saving? How would this guy know anything about that? Nothing made sense.

"If you want to see her alive, do as I say." The wimpy Mr. Lester had upped his game.

"Just who do you think you are making idle threats here on my ranch?"

Could he be the vandal or the elusive figure that Ivy and others thought they saw now and then? Damn! Too many questions. Troy needed answers and a plan before the situation got completely out of hand.

"I don't actually fly the Cessna," he lied. He'd need the freedom to take action against this crazy man, and he could not do that if he were busy at the controls. "Don't have my license. Not enough flying hours yet. I'll call my neighbor, Jack. He's a pilot."

Lester paced and appeared uncomfortable. "We're wasting time. This guy Jack better hurry."

Troy wanted to shake Lester, make him explain what the hell was going on. He didn't trust this guy, though

Ivy's note combined with the fact that no one had seen her since yesterday confirmed that she was in some kind of trouble.

"I'll taxi the plane out and get it ready for take-off. That much I can do."

Within a few minutes, the small plane was ready and waiting. Troy and Lester stood next to it as Jack, the pilot, screeched to a stop off to the side of the short, packed-dirt runway. He wasn't alone. A woman with a small child tagged along behind him trying to keep up with the man's fast pace. Both Troy and Lester said, "No! No way," at the same time.

Jack shook his head. "Sorry, I've got no choice here. I was about to take off in my own plane when you called. Got to get these two to the airport where a 747 is waiting for them. If you want me to fly your plane, they're coming along for the ride, and our second stop is Billings."

There was no time for Troy to explain the situation, but then, what would he explain? All he knew was that no one had seen Ivy since yesterday, and Lester seemed to know her location. "Everybody in. Buckle up."

Sitting in the co-pilot's seat, Troy exchanged troubled glances and whispered words with the pilot.

"This isn't good, is it?"

"No, Jack, I don't believe it is."

Lester took one of the two passenger seats, and the woman sat in the other with the boy on her lap. Nervous tension permeated the plane's small interior.

The engine roared, the woman bit her nails, the child cried, and Troy gave the command, "Take her up."

# MAYDAY, SEVEN KEYS & FAMILY TIES

## TWENTY

Troy left the co-pilot's seat and moved back a few feet so Lester could hear what he had to say. "Start talking. I'm running out of patience." His angry glare at this shell of a man intensified with each passing second.

Allowing the plane to leave the ground was a terrible idea. He and Jack should have tackled this crazed specimen when his idiotic demands first began. Where would they land? There were no runways in the middle of a forest or on the side of a mountain.

"Where are we going, Lester?"

"Uh... just head northwest." The man seemed uncertain. Sweat poured from his brow, and he looked ill. Motion sickness? Not all people do well flying in a small plane.

"That's not good enough. Try again, or we're turning this plane around."

"I wouldn't do that if I were you."

"Then spill the beans. Talk! What do you know about Ivy? Tell me now or we're taking the woman and her kid to Billings. We are not continuing on this wild—" Troy heard a noise. "Jack? Everything working properly up there?"

"10-4. Keeping my eye on the gas gauge, though. How much further out are we going?"

Troy had no idea, and he began to doubt Lester's ability to answer that question. Maybe this was nothing more than a bizarre fantasy orchestrated by a psychotic madman. Thoughts of pummeling him were diverted by a repetition of the noise he'd heard just moments ago, coming from the back of the plane. There it was again, a strange moaning sound in the small storage compartment. Had something come loose letting outside air seep in?

Unable to stand in the small plane, Troy crawled between the two seats and reached for the compartment door. "Oh, my god! It's Ivy." Seeing the blood and her semi-conscious state, he pulled out her curled up body as gently as possible, untied her hands, and examined her head wound. The bleeding had stopped, but he wanted to clean up the area around her cut. He couldn't bear to see her this way. He turned and faced Lester, his eyes boring into the weasel-like man's eyes. "You son-of-a-bitch! What have you done?" Troy violently yanked him from his seat and shoved him to the floor of the plane.

"Don't move. Not even your little finger if you know what's good for you."

The woman unbuckled her seatbelt, stepped around Lester, and knelt in the small space in front of the seat now occupied by Ivy. "I'll do what I can," she said, taking a water bottle and some tissues from her bag.

Grateful, Troy thanked her. "Right now, I need to deal with Lester."

With a weak smile, she added, "You do that."

"So, exactly what are we doing if not rescuing Ivy?" Incensed, Troy reached out to grab Lester's jacket, yearning to deliver some payback for what he'd done to the woman he loved.

Lester scooted backward. "I wouldn't do that if I were you. Don't touch me."

"You expect me to be a nice guy after what you did to Ivy?"

More than the man's face was dripping with sweat. Was he about to have a heart attack? Troy was desperate for immediate answers.

"You're right, we're not flying to her rescue. We're flying to our deaths."

"Turn the plane around, Jack," Troy shouted. "We're going home."

Lester's face turned bright red, his rapid breathing on the verge of hyperventilation. "We're all going to die unless you give me the location of the Seven Keys and the Seven Locks they fit into."

Stunned speechless, Troy felt as dazed and confused as Ivy appeared to be. What the hell? Was this some kind of sick joke? If so, no one was laughing. He glared at Lester, turned, and glanced out the window. At least they were heading in the right direction now. He sent the mother back to her seat to be with her child and sat on the floor beside Ivy.

"Darling, what happened?" he asked, trying to offer her some comfort.

Eyes wide open now, she frowned and put her hands to her head, but had no answer.

"You don't know what happened?"

"I went to your gym to work out and now I'm here with strangers, an upset stomach, a massive headache, and sore wrists." Moving her head carefully, she scanned the small, cramped surroundings, then looked up into Troy's eyes. "We're on speaking terms again?"

"Yes, darling, we are." He kissed her on the tip of her nose. She closed her eyes and sighed.

"Wait! Did Lester say something about seven keys?" She'd suddenly regained the ability to think.

"Yeah. Crazy, huh?" He noticed Ivy's frown had returned. Considering what she'd been through, he didn't give her question much thought. "What's your plan now, Lester? We're in a well-maintained plane with the best pilot in the area. It seems like you're the only one who should be worried. You're outnumbered, in case you hadn't noticed."

"It's not that simple. Give me the information about those keys and the locks and I'll text it to my boss. It's our only way to survive."

"There is no information to give you." Troy was done with this guy. No way would he be sucked into Lester's weird fantasy.

"Once I send the information and the treasure is bagged up and taken away, I'll receive a text with the mission accomplished code word, and we can all live happily ever after."

"Assuming I had treasure, why would I give it to you and some unknown, invisible man?"

Lester broke down and cried. He said it had been his job to find Troy's seven keys and seven locks, but he'd failed. Still sobbing, he choked out the words, "It wasn't supposed to end like this."

"Wait a minute," Ivy interrupted. "This guy, your boss, knew about Troy's seven keys?"

Troy just shook his head, unable to take any more of this insanity. "Hey, Jack, can you fly this plane any faster? Ivy needs medical attention." He knew increasing the plane's speed wasn't possible, but it felt good to ask.

Jack shouted back. "You're really beading up, Troy." In the past, when the two men flew together, they enjoyed bantering with pilot talk. Today, the words reserved for pilots served as a stress release to keep them calm during this dangerous, unexpected situation.

Troy shouted back, "No warm fuzzies for us today."

"It all started when he kidnapped my four-year-old granddaughter." Once Lester began talking, he couldn't stop the rush of information and the relief that came with finally confiding in someone else. "That animal said I'd never see her again if I didn't do this job for him. I didn't want to do any of this."

"And what exactly is *this*?" Troy wanted to pummel the man.

Lester kept talking and explained that his adorable granddaughter was in his charge while her mom, his daughter-in-law, was in Europe for a month. Now, he was supposed to blow up everyone including himself if he failed to text the location of the keys and all the wealth stashed at the ranch. "I'm not the bad guy. I'm really sorry, especially with the kid here and all."

The plane droned on. Ivy stood up with her hands on her hips and was the first to comment. "I don't believe you."

Troy chuckled. *That's my girl.* "Ivy, you do know you're high above the ground in a small plane, right?"

"I am?" She swallowed hard and sat back down in her seat.

Troy kissed her on the mouth and brushed the wisps of hair away from her eyes. "You're going to be fine. Just don't look down." He smiled, understanding her fear factor.

Looking up, he saw Lester standing slightly bent over and motionless, his jacket and shirt unbuttoned exposing an explosive vest that was attached to his body. Everyone gasped. The mother sank down in the small space behind her seat and reached around to hold her boy's hand.

"Believe me now, Miss Ivy?"

"Sure do. Who is this boss man you're working for?"

"He goes by Mr. V, but I've never seen him. He gets other guys to do his dirty—"

"The man on the phone. Your conversation after lunch yesterday. Of course, Mr. V."

"Why didn't you tell me about this strange conversation?" Troy demanded. He was beside himself.

"I tried. I looked all over the ranch for you and even left a note." Her exasperation was obvious. "Just tell him, Troy. Tell him where the money or whatever valuables you have are stashed." Her wide-eyed stare became a serious scowl. "Most people keep their money in the bank, you know."

Troy hesitated, then began. "All right. I'll play this game, but only for a few minutes. You can tell your Mr. V, or whoever that is, that to gather the loot they have to go into the main kitchen and then into the walk-in food cooler."

Lester fumbled with his phone, grunting and complaining. "I'm not so good at texting." He apologized, wiping his dripping forehead with his shirtsleeve. "We're not going to make it."

"Give me that," huffed Ivy, grabbing the phone from his inept, shaking hands. Her thumbs tapped rapidly on the screen as Troy talked, and Lester looked over her shoulder. The whole process took only several seconds.

"I thought I looked there," Lester whispered.

"Oh, so you're responsible for all the vandalism at the ranch too?"

He hung his head and nodded.

"Anything else?" She showed the entire text message to Lester. He gave a thumbs-up, and Ivy hit the send button. "What now?"

"We wait for the code word. When it comes, my granddaughter will be dropped off at the Kelly Library in the Englewood section of Chicago, and we can fly back to the ranch. See, it's a win for everyone."

"Then let's hope you charged your phone today. Locating the goods could take a while." Ivy had no confidence in this man. "Wouldn't want to miss your incoming text because your phone's battery went dead."

Lester looked down at the screen on his phone. No words were needed. The look on his face said it all.

Troy crouched down next to the pilot to check out the fuel situation. The two men exchanged disturbing glances. "I don't suppose you filed a flight plan."

"No. Didn't know how to file a last-minute flight plan to nowhere. I don't think we can make it back to the ranch on the gas we've got."

"You start looking for a place to land. I'll hope and pray for a miracle."

## TWENTY-ONE

L ester's phone showed that only 4% of his charge level remained, and Ivy knew they needed far more than *hope*. With lives at stake, she slipped from vacation mode into her no-nonsense work mode.

Staring at the man who'd put them all in such peril she said, "Let's pray that your Mr. V moves fast, finds what he came for, and gets the hell out," Ivy said, her tone unwavering.

Noticing Troy's worried expression, she insisted he share his thoughts. "Well...?" Why the hesitation? They needed any and all brainstorming possibilities.

Hunched over – he was too tall to stand erect in the small plane – he cleared his throat, sucked in a troubled breath, and blurted out, "No one will ever find the seven keys and the corresponding locks at the ranch. They are not there."

Lester spoke up. "This is bad, very bad. Mr. V will be mad as hell."

Confused, but slightly encouraged, Ivy had an idea. "Let's text a new message with the real location of the keys. If we hurry—"

"Forget about the keys," Troy interrupted. "They won't save us. We need to make it back to the ranch and catch this Mr. V by surprise, or at least get a message to one of my men."

Now Ivy was the one hesitating. "Uh, I might know what he looks like."

Troy radiated shock. "Really? Explain."

"That night in Denver when you were telling the bartender about some ranch and a unique seven-keys home security system – that was you, right? – a man was sitting at a table behind you and he seemed very interested in what you had to say."

"How do you know that?"

"I was there grabbing a bite to eat before driving home. It was a quiet night and only a few people were in the bar area. I was exhausted from a tough day at work, but also a bit bored until you began to tell your story. Do you tell it often?"

"Nope. That was the first time. About a year ago, I

visited my parents in Denver, and they told me of their anniversary plans to head up the mountain to visit the Baldpate Inn and its famous seven-keys mystery. Curiosity got the better of me, so I did some research.

"That night when you were in the bar, I got on a roll and told my own version of a seven-keys story. It was so good, I thought I'd tease my little brother with it someday if I ever saw him again." He never took his eyes off of Ivy as he spoke, and he seemed to be putting two and two together. "If we ever make it safely to the ground, we have more to discuss."

"All that seven-keys stuff was a joke? A fake story?" Lester weighed in, his whole body shaking. "The second Mr. V realizes the keys are not where you said they were, he'll blow up the vest remotely. He said he'd do that if there was any funny business, and this is funny business, deadly funny business. We're almost out of time. We're all going to die." He began to rock back and forth.

"Maybe not," Troy said, making eye contact with everyone but Jack, then focusing on Lester. "I'll just shove you and that vest right out the door. That's the simplest option. One casualty is better than six."

That was true, but still, there had to be another way out of this situation.

Troy continued, shouting over the noise of the engine.

"We can open the door without creating any additional flight problems, right Jack?"

"Yes, as long as everyone that intends to remain in the plane is buckled up tight. We still need a place to land, quickly. I'm running on fumes."

A new problem. One Ivy could not fix. Holding her breath, she focused on the vest issue and wondered whether Troy meant what he said. Lester looked as if he'd explode even if there were no vest attached to his body. She imagined the terror surging through him, went to his side, and patted his face. We're going to get this in-flight party started by taking off your vest, Lester."

"Thank you, Miss Ivy, but the vest will explode if I take it off." He pulled his shirt to the side so everyone could see the chain that attached the vest to his waist.

The woman who'd been silent since the trouble began asked, "You put that on yourself?"

"No, ma'am. One of Mr. V's muscle guys met me at the barn early this morning to give me the ether and the sleeping potion. Once we had Ivy unconscious and in the plane, he chained the vest to me and explained the whole plan."

Ivy gently ran her fingers over the vest. "It's mostly fabric, and fabric can be cut." She removed an odd-looking pair of scissors from the kangaroo pouch in her orange Denver Broncos hoodie. Together, she and Troy determine the safest places to make cuts in the fabric without touching or clipping any wires. During the close inspection of the vest, they agreed back alley thugs likely constructed it. "The lack of high tech expertise will make cutting around the chain easier. That's good, right?"

The look on Troy's face gave away his pessimistic thoughts. "Maybe, but it also makes the vest's response to our actions unpredictable.

Out of options and the cuts made, they told the shaking, white as a ghost man to kneel down. In spite of his skinny build, Lester's midsection was slightly larger than his shoulders, so over his head was the way to go. Slowly, carefully, they inched the vest upward until it no longer was part of the man's wardrobe. No one dared to breathe.

"Fasten your seatbelts!" Ivy shouted over the loud hum of the engines. "Lester, buckle up in the front seat."

Standing to the side of the plane's only exit with a seatbelt wrapped tightly, multiple times around his left arm, Troy looked down at the vest wedged between his feet and took several deep breaths. In a few seconds, he'd open the cabin door and hurl the killer vest from the plane.

"You fasten yours too, Ivy. Don't want you bailing out with the vest." He gave her a wink.

"You can do this, Troy." In spite of his wink, she saw worry written all over his face. The odds were not in his favor, and they both knew it. He was willing to give up his life to save theirs. "When it's done, we'll go back to the ranch and get on with the business of taking down Mr. V, the murderous thief." A smile, a nod, and a thumbs-up followed.

"Stay buckled up, Ivy, no matter what happens. Promise?"

She nodded weakly. Hoping to infuse the plane with good vibes and send encouragement to Troy, she asked the woman, the child, Lester, even Jack to countdown from three with her. Troy would make the toss on zero.

"Ready everybody? Ready Troy?"

He nodded.

"Three."

Troy locked eyes with Ivy and mouthed the words, I love you.

"Two."

When Troy unlatched the door, the air rushed out trying to take him and every loose item on the plane with it. Ivy shouted, "And I love you!"

He tossed the vest from the plane before giving the countdown crew a chance to finish. He'd saved the plane and its passengers, but could he save himself? In the process, his foot slipped and his lower half dangled from the open doorway. Ivy watched fearfully and called his name as if for the last time.

Watching him struggle, trying to pull his whole body back into the aircraft sent a knife-like pain through the middle of her heart. It couldn't end like this, could it? In the time it took to blink away a tear, Troy was in the plane shoving the cabin's door closed. He sank to the floor, exhausted.

The engine droned, and the passengers sighed with relief.

## TWENTY-TWO

The relief everyone felt after the vest was tossed from the plane quickly came to an end. A sudden, ear-shattering explosion brought back feelings of terror. They had expected the bomb to explode, but not so close to the plane. Now, pieces of shrapnel tore through its engine and lightweight body. The aircraft lurched sideways, and the passengers screamed.

"We've got a problem," Jack shouted. "Looking for a place to land!" He picked up the radio and called, "Mayday! Mayday!"

Troy thought the vest would explode on impact with the ground and not in the air. What went wrong? According to the guilty look on Lester's face, he knew the answer. "What gives, talk."

The man's entire body trembled, profuse sweat dripped as he tried to speak. "I guess Mr. V figured out I lied to him about the location of the keys and decided to blow us all up. That way he could take his time rounding up all of your stuff even if it wasn't the treasure. No way would he go home empty handed."

Troy's anger was red hot, over the top. His typical *cool and calm* personality was nowhere to be seen. "Why didn't you get help before this whole situation became so damn deadly?"

Lester sobbed. "I had to save my granddaughter."

"We all messed up." Ivy attempted to make the man feel better, though he didn't deserve any kindness. Not after what he'd done.

The engine sputtered and the plane began to lose altitude. *Thank God this is a prop plane.* If this had been the small jet he'd wanted to purchase last month, they'd be plummeting nose first down to the ground with no hope at all. At least this lightweight plane had the ability to glide for a while, though the pilot had little control due to the shrapnel damage.

"Jack, you buckled up?"

"Yes, my friend. Does your Cessna have a flight recorder on board?"

"Nope." Troy gave a thumbs down. "And we can't punch out of this one, can we?"

"Negative. Gonna fly her like a mud mover."

There were not enough seats for everyone, so Troy sat on the floor by Ivy. She shook her head, unbuckled her seatbelt, and stood up. Pointing at the empty seat, she said, "Sit!" He sat, then pulled her onto his lap and fastened the belt around them both. The plane would crash. No doubt about it. Would they live? Would they die? Either way, they'd do it together.

Jack did his best to keep the plane level, but the wings tipped from side to side, and the tail of the plane vibrated and shook violently. Finally, the engine sputtered one last time before quitting. They were in full glide now.

Lester prayed. The little boy cried. The woman stared out the window as if in a trance. Troy held Ivy with both arms wrapped tightly around her anticipating the pending impact. The plane rocked, then bounced. More scraping could be heard. They'd reached the tops of the trees. Ivy turned her head to say, "Troy, I'm so sorry. I never—" The plane with all its occupants slammed to the ground and cartwheeled through trees, over boulders. Then... silence.

---

IVY AWOKE to a faint whimpering sound and wondered if it came from her own throat. Her mind stalled and her thinking flickered on and off. Where was she? She saw nothing. Her head throbbed, her ears buzzed, and everything hurt. The world went dark again.

Troy's words brought her back. "Ivy? Come on, babe, you can do this." She felt her body turning and heard a gasp from above. She lay on the floor looking up at Troy. Her eyes struggled to focus as he spoke again. "We're alive! We survived the crash."

"Are you sure? I don't feel so good."

"Me either. But if we were *dead*, we wouldn't feel anything."

He'd made a good point. She struggled to sit up, but the plane's floor was no longer parallel with the ground and made the simple movement difficult. Accustomed to the site of blood, the red liquid on the floor didn't bother her until she realized it was her own.

She reached down and touched the dampness on her shirt. The presence of blood on her hands sent her reeling and was likely the reason for Troy's gasp. He stroked her face and kissed her forehead before lifting the blood-soaked fabric from her midsection.

"What's the verdict?" She had to know.

Her vision must have improved because she detected a twinkle in his eyes.

"What we have here is a good news, bad news situation."

"Please, the good news. I really need some good news."

Troy explained that the blood, though visibly shocking, seemed to be from multiple shallow cuts made by the seatbelt as it attempted to hold her tightly during impact. No sutures needed, just a damn good bandage.

Bracing herself, she asked for the bad news. Troy's eyes saddened. "The mother and Jack have not yet made a sound or moved a muscle. Maybe they're just unconscious, but I have a terrible feeling about them."

"Do you feel all right? You don't look like your usual self. You've got quite a few cuts and scrapes."

His hands traveled up to touch his face. Feeling the warm dampness, he stared at his palms tinged in red. "Guess I'll add this to my bad news list."

They smiled, weakly. The extent of their injuries was still to be determined. They'd fared better than the others, though. Ivy's past experience, the career she'd tried to escape from, kicked in and she began barking orders. "Triage first." And she ran to Jack who was slumped over sideways showing no signs of life. Looking up at Troy, she shook her head. "We'll leave his body here for now."

Still buckled in the co-pilot's seat, Lester moaned and groaned. A good sign, although a portion of the instrument panel was lodged against his leg. She would require Troy's help to move the man from the plane.

Holding the small boy's hand, Troy moved him away from his mother's side to allow Ivy to take a look. Checking her pulse, pupils, and visible injuries, she whispered, "Alive, but critical."

She asked Troy to carry the woman a safe distance from the plane and then come back to help with Lester. Ivy picked up the little boy. Soon, her three patients were settled on a soft bed of pine needles. One, near death. The other two in pain and frightened. And Jack? His body would be safer from hungry predators if left inside the plane.

"Troy, go back and see if you can find a first aid kit. We really need one."

He returned with a small, banged up kit, and Ivy went to work doing what she could. "It seems you've done this before," he said, watching her take charge.

Too busy trying to stop the blood flowing around her, she responded without looking up. "No, not exactly. Never treated plane crash victims out in the middle of nowhere." She confessed that she was an Emergency Medical Technician and a paramedic, jobs she was good at but had been running away from. "I need two sturdy sticks or branches about three feet long to immobilize Lester's broken leg. Then, two more twelve-inch branches to make a splint for the kid's arm."

"Got it. But when I return, I want to know all about you, Ivy. What other amazing facts have you kept from me?"

The mother stopped breathing. Ivy began chest compressions and continued until Troy return. "I'm not ready to give up on her. Not yet." Needing a short break to catch her breath, she showed him what to do before walking toward the plane in search of something, anything useful. Then, she stopped. "Hey, Lester. You still got that cell phone?"

Lester seemed unable to hear or comprehend her simple question. Instead, he sobbed and mumbled. "He told me this was a piece of cake, like taking candy from a baby. It wasn't."

Maybe she'd find it in the plane. Just as Ivy approached the wreckage, another ear-shattering explosion followed by high rising flames knocked her to the ground.

"Ivy!" Troy ran toward her and encircled her with his arms. "Thank God you weren't in the plane when it blew." She was shaken but had no new injuries. They embraced, but only for a moment. There was much to do, and nothing to do it with. All they had was an inferior first aid kit and the clothing on their backs. "The boy's mom didn't make it."

She reached up to gently caress his battered face. "Yeah, I'm not surprised. She was in bad shape, and now we need to move her further away from the living." Ivy was all business while Troy was visibly shaken, unfamiliar with trauma, blood, and death. "There is a tiny bit of good news here. Mr. V will assume we're all dead. That could work to our advantage." They hurried back to Lester, the boy, and the dead woman.

While Troy moved the boy's mother closer to the wreckage, Ivy did everything possible for her patients. She wrapped the bleeding flesh with the sleeves she'd torn from her sweatshirt and immobilized injured bones using the sticks Troy had gathered and the laces from her athletic shoes. What a rag-tag, pitiful sight.

Lester was in no condition to be moved, and the boy was weak, his condition yet to be determined. Either one of them could have internal injuries, so their best option was to wait for help. The ranch was probably the closest slice of civilization. But how far was that? Five miles? Ten? Their survival depended on Ivy and Troy's ability to get to the ranch ASAP and return with a well-equipped medical team and a way to transport the injured.

"Lester, the boy needs your help." She set the child next to him. "Huddle together to keep warm. Do not move from this spot. Got it?" He nodded.

"Sweetie, what's your name?"

"My name is Billy and I'm a very good boy. I will do what you say to do."

Troy whispered in her ear, "At least one of them seems to know what's going on. Just wish he was a little older."

Ivy knelt down and kissed the boy's cheek. "I'm sorry about your mom, but stay right here. Don't go over to her. Okay?"

"That's not my mom. She's the lady taking me to stay with uncle Bob in Ory-gon."

"Where is your mom or your dad?" The moment the words came out, she wished she could take them back.

"I never had a dad and mom's... gone."

Ivy's heart broke as she hugged him gently. Apparently, in his short life, he'd already experienced more than his share of trauma. Both physical and emotional.

Troy gave the boy an affectionate pat on the head and said, "Try not to worry. We will come back for you. Can you be brave for a few hours?" Billy nodded. Troy grabbed Ivy's hand and they ran, blood oozing from their own unbandaged injuries.

Troy assured Ivy that he knew the general direction they should travel and that certain landmarks would aid the accuracy of their trek. It wasn't long before their journey proved to be more hazardous than expected. Racing over rolling rocks, slippery boulders, and fallen tree trunks was challenging enough without the streams, hills, and valleys they encountered.

Highly motivated to save Lester and Billy and to give Mr. V a hefty dose of his own evil medicine, they pushed through their pain. They traveled as a team, helping each other every grueling step of the way. They were going for the gold. Nothing else would do.

Exhausted, they stopped briefly at one of the flowing streams they'd jumped across and took a drink. They could not afford to add dehydration to their list of problems and would deal with any stomach issues that might arise later. Catching his breath, Troy attempted to speak a few encouraging words.

"The trip back to the wreckage will be much faster and easier with the help of the horses and some off-road vehicles." He estimated they'd traveled approximately one mile in about twelve minutes. If the plane had gone down ten miles from the main house at the ranch, they would arrive in less than two hours. If they were further out... neither spoke of that possibility.

---

"WE'RE ALMOST HOME," Troy said, recognizing the subtle landmarks of the outer edges of the ranch property. "We should assume Mr. V and his posse – no, his goons, posse is too nice a word for our uninvited gangsters – are still looking for my money."

They walked toward the main buildings scanning their surroundings with the caution and alertness of two deer during hunting season. Suddenly, Troy stopped and changed their direction. "I'm sure our predators are armed. We should be too."

The plan was to locate a gun, any gun, at the livery stable and find a few wranglers to be their back-up now and rescuers a little later. Not much luck with that. No wranglers, not even any horses. The corral gates stood wide open. *Dammit!*

They'd hoped to find more, but at least they were no longer empty-handed. They left the stables, Troy with a handgun, Ivy with a tire iron, and continued their search for the evil ones.

"Maybe we'll stumble upon some good guys along the way," Ivy whispered, looking up into his eyes. "Still love me?"

Troy gave her pretty face a soft kiss. "More than ever."

Ivy held the tire iron like a spear, stabbing at the air, ready to do some damage. Troy shook his head. "Love your enthusiasm, but we need the element of surprise. It's strangely quiet right now, too quiet. Any door bashing or window shattering would alert Mr. V of our presence."

Every door, in every building they tried to enter, was locked. Odd. These doors were never locked during daylight hours. And where were the guests? His staff? The horses? Did Mr. V force his wranglers to take all the horses, guests, and staff on an extra-long ride? Didn't seem logical that his men would react passively and go along with orders from some low-life, city gangster. Knowing his staff, a couple of his wranglers might relish the excitement of a fight. He could imagine them saying, "Bring it on!" followed by a string of four-letter words.

Finally, an unlocked door, the kitchen's rarely used side entrance. Troy, with his gun ready, and Ivy gripping her short, but solid spear-like weapon, entered slowly, silently. They found the contents of the stainless steel, industrial-size refrigerator, shelves, and closets scattered across the floor, which made treading lightly a challenge.

The kitchen, though obviously trashed, seemed clear of any lurking, mortal danger. Troy picked up the receiver off the wall phone. Just as he'd assumed, the phone was dead. Likely, all the ranch phone lines had been cut.

Troy pointed at the interior door to the hallway that connected the kitchen to The Lodge. He breathed a sigh of relief remembering that last week he'd insisted there be no squeaky doors anywhere on the ranch property. Still, getting to that door silently felt like traveling across a minefield.

The hallway was dark, and they didn't dare attract attention by flipping on the lights. From Troy's vantage point, only seven short steps in, he saw a man crouched further down the hallway holding a... a meat cleaver. They froze. Ivy gasped. The man turned and put a finger to his lips signaling for silence.

## TWENTY-THREE

Troy squinted in the dim light. "Trace?" Shocked, he couldn't believe his eyes. The crouching man in the dark hallway was his younger brother who lived in Colorado.

"Troy? You're alive?"

Ivy peeked out from behind Troy, and they both nodded.

He hadn't seen his younger brother in years. Why was he here now? He had to have some answers. He motioned for Trace to follow him back to the kitchen, then pointed at the walk-in cooler. Once all three were inside, out of earshot, they exchanged a few words.

"Well, brother, you showed up just in time for a fight." Troy glanced down at the huge knife. "A *gun* fight. What do you know about what's going on here?"

"Nothing that makes sense, but a big boss man is making himself at home in The Lodge while an Indian named Kitchi went out to make sure your staff and guests remained locked up. The guy must have thought Kitchi was harmless and not too bright because he let him move around freely. After he came back and reported everyone was where they should be, the big boss man told him to go and help round up all your treasure. You have treasure?"

Troy shook his head and blew out a frustrated breath. "No. I'll explain later."

Trace went on. "The last thing he said to the Indian was that you were dead and he would be too if he didn't comply. I saw him face-to-face as he hurried past me in the hallway likely on his way to hunt for treasure. He said nothing to me. Probably thought I was one of the bad guys."

"The big boss man, as you call him, goes by Mr. V. He's a gangster from Chicago who tried to kill six people by blowing up my plane. So far, two are dead, and if we don't get help to the crash site ASAP, the two remaining survivors might die too." Troy paused momentarily and passed his fingers through his hair. "Is he alone? Any goons to take the bullets for him?"

"I haven't seen anyone else. Doesn't mean others aren't here. I just arrived about thirty minutes ago and parked myself in this dark hallway until I could figure out what was up."

"Trace, do you think he knows you're here?"

"Probably not. After seeing the emptiness and unusual quietness of the ranch I knew something was wrong, so I kept out of sight."

"Good, here's the plan. I'll go in as the ghost of... myself, and tell him a story. Catch him off guard. Scare the—" He looked at Ivy.

"Really? Come on, at this point, a four-letter word is the least of my worries. Hi Trace, I'm Ivy." She reached out and shook his hand. "I'm surprised Kitchi didn't come back."

"I can only assume that he's smart enough to know Mr. V would be less than pleased if he came back empty-handed. Although his hands were definitely full when he left."

"What's that supposed to mean?" Troy asked, his frustration building.

"You know, it could've been a dog, but I swear he was holding a squirming coyote pup." Three sets of eyes glanced around studying each other. Two with questioning looks, but Ivy's eyes seemed almost joyful.

"Interesting, huh? Well... you got a phone, Trace? I'll go outside and call for some real law enforcement back-up, an ambulance or two, and maybe a helicopter," she said, and held out her hand.

Troy felt a wave of worry crash against his brain, or was it his heart? "I'd like it better if you stayed in here."

"I'll hide behind the dumpster and speak softly. I'll be okay."

This brave, beautiful woman's idea was solid, but how could he protect her if they were separated? He couldn't chance losing her now. He loved her and he needed her.

She stood holding out her hand until Trace relinquished his cell phone. "Calling for back-up is a good idea, but stay in here to make your call. We don't know how many goons Mr. V brought with him, but those guys in denim that the wranglers saw yesterday are likely still around."

"Guys in denim?" Ivy frowned.

"A new development. I'll explain later. Make your call, but do it from here. It's not safe outside." Troy and Trace stepped from the walk-in cooler leaving Ivy behind.

"Got an extra gun, Troy? I'm not feeling safe enough with a meat cleaver. Rather not get that close to a murderer."

"Afraid not, but I can get you a larger one, and I'll throw in a solid metal mallet capable of beating the toughness from any kind of flesh." Troy chuckled and gave his brother the gun and a long overdue hug. They shared a few final words before each headed to his self-assigned position. The McAllister brothers had a plan.

The nefarious Mr. V looked up when Troy entered through the hallway. He sat in one of the large leather chairs, relaxed with his legs crossed at the knee, sipping straight from a bottle of Jim Beam. "And just who might you be, cowboy? No, wait, let me guess." The man laughed at the sight of Troy standing there with a meat cleaver in one hand and a mallet in the other. "Bet you're nothing more than kitchen help," the vile man snarled. "Only a hair better than that small, half-blind Indian."

That did it! How dare he speak those words about the wisest man in Montana? It took all of Troy's patience to keep from using the mallet right then and there. Knowing Ivy was calling for backup and Trace would make his appearance any minute, he proceeded with absolute confidence and made as much noise as possible. Trace had to unlock and open The Lodge's front door without being heard. Troy pounded his weapons together over his head like an ancient warrior, shouting, "You're trespass-ing. You've caused great damage to my ranch and you've murdered my friends. You're going—"

"Then you must be Troy. Hmm, that's an interesting

twist." A maniacal laugh spewed from his throat. "What happened? Did you miss your flight?"

"What's your purpose here?" Troy asked, knowing the answer, but stalling while Trace got into position. A few more details from this murdering criminal could be useful.

"With time no longer of the essence, I'm enjoying *your* ranch. Maybe I'll ride one of your horses while waiting for my little search party to gather the hidden keys that will unlock much of the McAllister wealth, jewels, you name it. With the help of your Indian friend, they will find it. It will soon be mine, all mine. Then I, alone, will be on my way."

Troy's hate for this evil man deepened with each passing second. "I see. That sounds ominous."

"Oh, it is. But it gets much worse. Here comes the best part," he said with a smirk. He was toying with Troy, dragging out and enjoying the inevitable. "I'm afraid your timing is terrible. All of the witnesses exploded in midair. Did you know about that? But now here *you* are. You're just another witness in my way, and I can't leave any witnesses behind. I'm sure you understand." Mr. V calmly held up the gun he'd kept by his side and pointed it at Troy. "Any last words?"

Finally, it was two against one. Troy liked those odds.

"A few. How do you feel about the gun pointed right at the back of your head?"

———————

THERE WAS no cell service inside the walk-in cooler, so Ivy followed her original plan. If she had her way, she'd run straight to her cabin to check on her puppy, but saving human lives had to come first. She crouched down behind the dumpster and tapped 9-1-1 on the cell phone.

"9-1-1, what's your emergency?"

"We need help!" she whispered. "There's been a plane crash, injuries, murders..."

Before she finished her plea for assistance, a man grabbed her roughly by the hair and another squeezed her wrist forcing her hand to give up the phone. "Hey, that's my phone and I want it back," she said as the two men wearing denim coveralls shoved her toward the kitchen door. "Nice outfits." One of the men slapped her across the face.

"Just shut up and do as you're told. Mr. V is gonna be in a nasty mood when he learns all we found was a smart ass woman."

Furious, Ivy kicked and thrashed determined to free herself from these two accomplices as they made their way through the kitchen and down the hallway that connected it to The Lodge. She nicknamed her stupid-looking assailants Mutt and Jeff, and told them so. After receiving another slap, she delivered a swift kick to one of their shins.

Entering The Lodge, all three seemed surprised by what they saw there. Troy stood firm holding a heavy meat mallet like a hatchet he was about to throw in one hand and an odd-looking knife in the other. Mr. V sat in the big leather chair with Trace standing directly behind him aiming a gun at the back of his head. And Ivy? She felt the cold metal of two gun barrels pressed against her skin. One on her temple, the other on her neck.

Three armed and dangerous bad men, two somewhat armed good men, and one innocent hostage equaled a six-person standoff. *This will make one wild and crazy story, if I live to tell it.*

Ivy looked directly at Mr. V, took a deep, calming breath, and prayed she'd find the right words to put an end to this deadly situation. "I don't know what you can accomplish here. There is no treasure. No seven-keys locking up Troy's wealth. You fell for that ridiculous story?" She winced, knowing she'd fallen for it too.

Did he believe her? Was that a look of regret on the madman's face? Maybe, maybe not. His somewhat blank expression faded and was replaced by insane anger and pure evil. Her own rage superseded her calming tone.

"You killed people today, nice people. You won't get away with that."

"Ivy," Troy shouted. "Relax darlin'. We've got this."

Mr. V rose to his feet, Trace's gun still ready to put a hole in the man's head. "You're Ivy?" She nodded. "You missed your flight too? What the hell is going here?" He glared at his hitmen.

"We did everything you said to do. Drugged the girl, put her in the plane, and strapped the explosives to Lester. We saw them take off."

"Two of the people you say were on the plane – the same plane that I detonated in midair – are standing right here in this room. So, I repeat, what the hell is going on?"

No one spoke, and unless a little divine intervention materialized, a distraction was critical. This standoff wouldn't last forever. Triggers would be pulled, and people would die. But what could be done?

Ivy noticed Trace's raised eyebrows, his wide-open eyes, and the tilt of his head. Interesting. She took that as a signal of some kind. A plan. She subtly followed the tilt of his head, which seemed to lead to the far end of the bar. Had Troy noticed too? Something was about to happen.

All at once, the piercing sound of bullets flying and glass shattering did the trick. Mr. V's eyes snapped toward the far end of the bar where bottles of whiskey and wine exploded. His goons also turned to look as broken glass flew through the air and multi-colored liquid splashed in all directions. For a second, the sounds, the colors, and the scent of gunpowder mimicked fireworks on the 4th of July.

Trace jumped Mr. V, knocked the gun from his hand, and kicked it toward Ivy. He then dealt a heavy blow to the evil man's head rendering him unconscious and tied his hands behind his back with a bandana from his pocket.

At the same time, Troy rushed toward Ivy and bashed one of the men holding her hostage with the metal mallet. The remaining man, shocked and confused by the sudden commotion, stepped a few feet away from Ivy. She dropped to the ground and grabbed the gun that had been kicked her way and pointed it up at the man. To her dismay, his gun was aimed down at her. *Here we go again. Another standoff.*

Mr. V and Jeff, injured and unconscious, were no longer a threat. "Give up, you're surrounded," she shouted. The guy she'd name Mutt had two guns pointing at his face, but she wasn't out of the woods yet. His gun was aimed right at her chest, and he looked like he'd use it.

"Oh, yeah? How 'bout we go out together in a blaze of glory? We'll shoot each other. Let's countdown from three to zero." Mutt, crazy and every bit as evil as Mr. V, smiled maliciously showing his disgusting brown teeth.

She had an idea that would stall for time. "Nope, that's not enough drama. We can do better than that. I know, let's start our countdown from ten," she said slowly, looking the man straight in the eye.

Would this deranged, stupid goon pull the trigger before reaching zero? Could Ivy pull the trigger in this kill or be killed situation? She prayed the gun in Trace's hand was loaded. How many bullets did each gun hold? So many questions, so many scenarios whirled around in her brain. She hadn't planned on playing games, especially not Russian roulette.

## TWENTY-FOUR

The countdown began. They'd only reached the number seven when Kitchi and the wranglers burst through The Lodge's main door. The man Ivy called Mutt looked up at the commotion, giving Troy and Trace a brief advantage. They tackled and disarmed him quickly.

Cody and his wranglers gladly took it upon themselves to deal with Mr. V and his goons, tying them up securely and checking for additional weapons. Trace and Kitchi seemed to be deep in conversation making plans for the rescue.

Troy took Ivy in his arms and held her closer and tighter than ever before. Shocked and exhausted, but glad to be alive, they left The Lodge to briefly distance themselves from the murdering criminal and to clear their minds while several of the wranglers rounded up the items and horses needed for the rescue. Troy led the way with purpose in his walk.

"Where are we going?" Ivy asked, eyeing him with suspicion.

"To your cabin. Don't you want to check on him?"

"You know?"

Troy nodded, looking serious. "I do now. Kitchi and Trace kind of let the cat out of... I mean they spilled the beans, don't you think?" His charming smile had been hidden away since the fateful plane ride, but now it was back in full force. "We don't have much time. Show me this pup that's got you wrapped around his little paw."

Ivy smiled, her aches and pains almost forgotten. "Well, he's a *she*, and her name is Shadow. You're going to love her too."

---

THEY HEARD the yipping as they approached the cabin's door. "Sounds like Shadow is in need of some company," stated Troy. Ivy hurried inside and scooped the tiny pup into her arms. The yipping softened to a whimper.

"Do you want to hold her?" She handed off the pup before Troy could respond to her question.

He held her close, examining every inch of the tiny fluff ball. "Son-of-a-gun. She really is a coyote, but that makes no sense. Coyotes give birth in May or June. Only in rare cases does this happen in early July. Shadow can't be more than seven or eight weeks old, which means she was born mid-August."

All three lay on the bed taking a brief moment to relax. Two of the three tried to recoup their strength. They were the leaders of the search and rescue party that would head out soon. The pup snuggled between them. Solving the coyote pup mystery would have to wait. There was life-saving work to be done. Troy played with the pup while Ivy changed into some warmer, bloodless clothing.

"Did you have time to make your 9-1-1 call?"

"I'd just begun talking with the dispatcher when Mutt and Jeff took the phone away. I'd said something about murders and injuries and that we needed help. You know the rest."

"But what happened to the phone?"

"One of the guys tossed it into the dumpster."

That gave Troy a glimmer of hope. Someone might track the phone's location and send help to the ranch, though not to the crash site and its remaining survivors. No, they couldn't wait until help arrived.

They took Shadow out for a quick potty break, gave

her some food, and filled her water dish. Ivy placed her on the blanket in her cozy, all-purpose box. When the pup whimpered, Troy said, "Kitchi will take good care of her while we're gone." Time was of the essence. They had to get going. "Ivy, grab a warm coat. The temperature is already dropping, and we might not get home before dark."

---

THE LODGE SERVED as the command center and makeshift jail. By consensus, it was decided that Troy, Ivy, and two of the wranglers would make up the rescue team. Kitchi, Cody, and the other wrangler would stay behind and continue the efforts to reach law enforcement and emergency medical assistance while making sure Mr. V, Mutt, and Jeff remained tied up tight. Kitchi understood he was also the protector of the coyote pup.

Trace made a call to someone named Hannah. From what Troy overheard, his brother couldn't bring himself to tell her what had happened here in Montana. Instead, he inquired about how she was doing back home in Colorado.

Troy hurried to the corral expecting to hop on a quad and round up some horses. Many of them, however, had wandered back on their own. It was time for their oats.

Luckily, the wranglers were way ahead of him. They'd saddled up four trail horses for the team to ride and two pack horses to carry the food, water, blankets, and medical supplies. Last stop before heading out, back to The Lodge, where Ivy waited for them.

She stood in the doorway holding up a satchel. "Kitchi's contribution to our medical supplies. Dried dandelion roots for pain and dogwood bark for fevers. He really wanted to come with us." Then, she called out some parting words to the team left behind. "If you find a working phone, demand a medevac chopper. Even if it can't land, it will be able to spot the crash site quicker and easier than we can."

Troy helped her mount up thinking all the while how much he loved this talented, wise woman. She was tough too. All banged up and never uttered a word of complaint.

Out of the blue, her previous comments regarding the attributes of his Life Path number came to mind. According to numerology, he was destined to have incredible strength and psychic ability. A Seven was the most magical of all numbers. He liked the sound of that and hoped it carried some truth, nevertheless, he silently prayed for a little divine intervention.

Finding Lester and the boy would not be easy. The trail they'd left while hurrying south toward the ranch would be hard to find, if not impossible. All Troy really knew was to head north.

---

ADRENALIN RUSHED through Ivy's body, but not in the usual way. She was in her element, her area of expertise when it came to saving humans in distress, but the remote location and their dire situation made her feel hopeless. She'd keep that thought to herself.

Troy led the way and Ivy followed as each wrangler ponied a packhorse. Reaching the north end of the ranch's property line was quick and easy. For the next half hour or so the team forged ahead with confidence. Only the sounds of one wrangler whistling a tune now and then and the soft clopping of horses' hooves on the rolling terrain could be heard. They were on a mission, a solemn one. The lives of two people were in their hands.

Up ahead was a densely forested area with boulders, hills, and streams. Ivy moved her horse forward to ride side by side with Troy. "Refresh my memory. What landmarks are we looking for? I don't recall much of our trip from the crash site down to the ranch."

"I was about to ask you the same question. So far, the sun's position has helped me lead us in a northerly direction, but we need to get specific if we're ever going to find them."

They rode in silence for a while, deep in thought, trying to recall anything they'd notice on their dash to the ranch. Ivy rattled off her short list of memories: a rock formation that resembled a snowman, an abandoned beaver den in one of the larger streams, a fallen tree trunk forming a bridge over a small creek, and an old fire ring likely made by a camper or hunter years ago.

"I'm impressed. We'll keep an eye out for all of those things." Troy's recollections were fewer, but hopefully easier to spot: a tall stand of a dozen or more dead pine trees in a clearing the size of his private, horse-breeding pasture, and a rock wall with one large, charred tree leaning up against it.

"If only we'd been resourceful and left a trail like Hansel and Gretel."

"You're brilliant. We did leave a trail. A blood trail."

They all took a short break, sharing their thoughts and ideas regarding landmarks. The wranglers wore skeptical looks. One added, "Okay, but there's no way we'll see a tiny drop of blood on the ground."

"You could be right about that," Ivy agreed, "but I remember touching my blood-soaked shirt and wiping the sweat from my bleeding face. My hands were often covered in blood. At times I needed to grab onto a branch, tree trunk, or a boulder to keep my balance. The smudge or handprint left there would be much larger than a drop."

Everyone nodded and mounted up. Four sets of eyes had work to do. They spotted the charred tree first. Whoops and hollers rang out. So far, so good. Within ten minutes, Troy spotted the Snowman Rock and estimated they were halfway to their destination.

Unfortunately, the sun had dipped below the tree line lowering the temperature and casting shadows. Any blood smears would be invisible in the dim light, and Lester and the boy's chances of survival lessened as the air grew colder. They were running out of time.

"Hey, boss, maybe we should split up, spread out."

Troy and Ivy whispered about the pros and cons of the wrangler's idea. They agreed the plan would cover more ground, but Troy insisted that he and Ivy stay together. Ivy insisted they remain within shouting distance of each other and call out their names every few minutes. "Let's give that a try before we spread out. We can't take the chance of losing each other."

"Troy."

"Ivy."

"Stan."

"Rick."

Ivy had one more idea. The first team member to spot

the crash site, Lester, or the boy would holler the code words *GOT GOLD*. They'd continue this system until they found Lester and Billy, or total darkness rendered the search pointless. Admittedly, desperation was becoming the unspoken word of the hour.

After four more name call-outs, Ivy said, "I'm getting a faint whiff of smoke. I'm sure of that."

"You've got a keen sense of smell, darlin'. Can't be a fire, even I'd smell that."

"Maybe one of your wranglers lit up a cigarette."

Troy shook his head. "Can't be that either. Neither Rick nor Stan smoke."

"Yeah, but Lester does!"

Troy called out his name over and over while Ivy led the way toward the faint scent. Not a word of reply came from the injured man. Discouraged, they pushed ahead. Before long, even the smell of smoke had faded. Maybe it only existed in Ivy's wishful imagination.

Troy stopped his horse suddenly and put up his hand to signal Ivy to stop too. "What? Did you see something?" she asked.

He put a finger to his lips, then tapped his ear. A faint, tiny voice. They both heard it.

"I'm here. I'm over here." That had to be Billy.

"Got gold! Got gold!"

## TWENTY-FIVE

The little boy cried out, "Wow! Horses!" Moving closer, Troy saw that his face was stained with tears. He sat holding his arm and smiled in spite of the pain. Lester didn't move or open his eyes.

The rescue team dismounted. Ivy ran to Billy who'd remained next to the injured man. "Are you doing all right?" She took his pulse and examined his arm. Vitals seemed okay, but his skin was warm to the touch. A small child who'd been sitting still for hours surrounded by cold air should feel cool. An infection was likely.

Troy brought over the first aid kit and Kitchi's pack of remedies and set them down next to Ivy. "Thanks. Why don't you take Billy to see the horses? I need some time with Lester, first."

"Yes, ma'am." He'd notice that she walked slightly bent over, holding her midsection after dismounting. Kneeling down, he whispered into her ear, "Are you okay?" He kissed that ear waiting for her answer.

She turned and looked up, her face forming a weak smile. "I'll be fine. I'm just tired, that's all." He hoped she was telling the truth. "How about you, cowboy?" she added. "You're walking with a limp."

"Just stiff and achy. Nothing a good soak in the spa can't fix." He scooped Billy up in his arms and they headed over to where the horses were temporarily tethered.

Stan and Rick hung out with the horses waiting for further instructions from Troy.

"Which one is yours?" Billy asked Troy.

"The brown one with the black mane."

"Can I pet him?"

"Sure. He'd like that."

"What's his name?"

"Tracker. Do you want to sit on him?" Billy's eyes opened wide. Troy took that as a 'yes.'

Standing by the horse's side, he motioned Stan and Rick to come closer. He imparted the worst news first. They'd be spending the night there. No way could they safely return to the ranch in the dark. Unfortunately, they'd been in such a hurry to get back to Lester and

Billy, they hadn't planned for that scenario. Though they had plenty of supplies, they lacked any type of shelter.

"Go ahead and remove the saddles and hobble the horses. Then get a good fire going and collect enough wood to keep it burning all night. After that, put on your creative hats and build some shelters."

Troy assigned himself the job of cook. First, he'd keep Billy occupied until Ivy finished checking Lester and felt she could focus on the boy. "Do you know how we found you?" The boy shook his head. "Ivy said she smelled smoke. Pretty clever of Lester to light up a cigarette."

Billy shook his head. "All the man did was cry. I cried too."

The child's face held a look of shame just for crying. Troy searched for a few comforting words. "That's understandable. Lots of scary things happened."

Still sitting on the horse's back, Billy said, "I know I'm not supposed to play with fire. The cigarette was poking out of his pocket and then I saw the lighter on the ground. Sorry I broke a rule. I lighted the cigarette."

Troy lifted him from the horse and held him. "It's a good thing you broke that rule because it saved your life."

Billy buried his head on Troy's chest. "You're not mad at me?"

"Nope. I'm proud of you. Are you hungry?"

"Yes, sir."

"Let's go find some food."

Billy chewed on a granola bar while Troy sifted through the edible supplies. Ivy joined them by the fire. "I'm going to need some boiled water. Can you do that for me, Troy?"

"Sure. Some boiling water coming up."

They both worried about Lester's deteriorating condition and kept their voices low as they discussed their options. "Billy could ride with you, but I don't see a suitable way to get Lester back to the ranch."

"We could construct a travois, but the terrain is too rugged. I doubt the man would survive the rough ride even if it were possible."

"Well, we can't leave him here."

It seemed Lester's only way out of there would be on a homemade stretcher, hand carried by members of the rescue team. Ivy's immediate plan for him included removing the splint so she could give his leg a thorough cleansing and making some dogwood bark tea to help with fevers and infection. The jury was still out on giving both of her patients a few dried dandelion roots to chew on. Troy eyed the roots with curiosity and thought he'd try a few. What harm could come from a common weed?

With primitive lean-tos built and the horses fed and watered, they all gathered around the fire. Dinner consisted of dried meat, nuts, apples, and snack packs of cheese and crackers. The only beverage was water or dogwood bark tea. Most opted for the water. Billy tried the tea. "This is gross!" he blurted out, then slapped his hand over his mouth as if he expected to be scolded.

"I'll second that," Stan agreed. The boy smiled shyly.

Lester ate and drank a little. His eyes were open, and he answered simple questions with a slight shake of his head, even a few single-syllable words – all encouraging signs. Still, he hadn't moved yet, and Ivy was afraid to move him. The wranglers set up a lean-to over him right where he sat.

Troy suggested everyone try to get some sleep. Rick and Stan rolled up in their blankets and used their saddles as headrests. Troy, Ivy, and Billy lay down under a large lean-to. The boy fell asleep right away. The adults doubted they'd sleep at all, but at least their bodies would get some needed rest.

The fire crackled, then sizzled. Sizzled? What the heck? No. No. Nooooo! Raindrops fell from the jet-black sky. Could this rescue be any more difficult? Troy's thought was punctuated with bright bolts of light illuminating the sky. Lightning, followed by a deep rumbling sound. *Dammit! There's my answer.* A thunderstorm was far worse than rain.

The lightning became brighter and the rumbling

louder. The horses stomped and snorted. Troy, Ivy, Rick, and Stan wiped the rain from their eyes as they looked skyward mesmerized like characters in a science-fiction movie gazing up at a UFO.

Either aliens were landing on earth or – help had arrived! The four adults cheered. The lights and the thundering noise came from a helicopter. They watched a couple of first responders climb down to the ground, one at a time, via a rescue ladder. They carried medical supplies on their backs. Several large canvas bags followed.

"Thank God you're here. We didn't know if anyone would find us."

"We were about to head back and start fresh tomorrow when we saw your fire," said one of the men. "Our pilot can't land here, but we noticed a suitable spot about one mile to the southwest. He'll come back at first light."

The two paramedics gave additional medical aid to Lester and Billy, while the wranglers opened the bags. Tents! They contained three small, but substantial tents. Next, a lightweight stretcher came down from the chopper, and then a third person, a woman, was lowered to the ground.

"The pilot needs to head back, but these guys can stay

to help transport the injured to the pick-up spot in the morning."

Something wasn't right. "Why can't you take the injured out now?" Troy wanted an answer.

The other man stepped up. "This isn't a real medevac chopper. None were available. This was the best we could do, and it doesn't come with a basket. From this location, your injured would need to be lifted in a basket. Anything less would be too risky."

The man's statement made sense, but Troy wasn't happy about it. Turning to the woman, he asked, "Who are you? And what is your purpose here?"

"I'm Agent Bauer with the FBI. The perpetrators involved in the recent criminal activity at your ranch crossed state lines. I flew up with the medics to deliver some news and to cuff the man named Lester."

Ivy placed herself between the FBI agent and her patient. "That's not going to happen. He's a good man who was just trying to save his granddaughter's life. He is seriously injured and can't be moved right now." After Ivy invited the agent to spend the night at the campsite, the woman backed off with her tough talk and agreed to wait until Lester was resting comfortably in a hospital. Then, she'd resume her questioning and, likely, arrest him.

Facing Troy, she said, "Rest assured that Frankie

Valasto, I believe you call him Mr. V, is in custody along with one of his men. A team will arrive at your ranch tomorrow to speak with your guests and staff members. I'm afraid the guests will need to leave after giving their statements. The ranch will be a crime scene for a while. And just so you know, Valasto's other thug is dead. A blow to his head may be the cause. We'll talk more about that later," she said, eyeballing Troy.

"A crime scene with yellow tape and all?" Ivy's creative mind was suddenly on overload.

"Yes, just like on TV." All business, she turned and headed back to the rescue seat that would lift her up to the chopper. "One more thing. The man named Kitchi asked me to tell you that Shadow's mystery has been solved. He said you'd understand."

The rain stopped, and the chopper carrying the FBI agent disappeared into the darkness.

## TWENTY-SIX

The sky was a deep shade of gray when Ivy awoke to the sound of activity and the smell of coffee. She'd slept, after all. Troy began to stir, and Billy mumbled in his sleep about horses and his new mommy. Odd. But everything was odd lately.

Ivy sat up knowing there was much work to be done, but groaned in pain and laid back down needing a few more minutes to summon her strength. Her thoughts drifted to yesterday morning. Less than twenty-four hours ago she was in a warm, comfortable bed snuggled up with her puppy. Today, every inch of her body hurt, the stiffness almost unbearable. She knew she'd never be quite the same physically or emotionally.

Her plan to get away from emergency medical issues had backfired beyond belief, and her anticipated hope that spending time at the ranch writing a novel would take away her sadness had failed. These two weeks were to be the beginning of her reinvented, fabulous new life. She'd never felt so far from fabulous. Whining wasn't her style, but this morning, inside her head, there was a whole lot of whining going on. *Snap out of it!* she scolded.

Troy was awake now. He helped her stand, then held her in his arms in full view of the others. "Mmm. That feels good." They stepped closer to the warmth of the fire. Stan handed them each a Styrofoam cup filled with strong, black coffee. It smelled better than it tasted. Nevertheless, the hot drink warmed their insides and seemed to give them a much-needed jolt of energy.

"I meant what I said in the plane," he whispered into her tousled hair waiting for her comment.

Ivy took another sip of the hot drink pondering whether or not she wanted to know what he was referring to. "Many things were said when we were up in the air in the small plane. Refresh my memory. I need a hint."

He smiled and gently caressed her face. Her beauty shined through in spite of her injuries and exhaustion. "Okay, no guessing games. I'll get right to it. I'm in love with you, Ivy."

She did remember. They'd each said I love you while up in the plane, but at the time, they both expected to die. "Did you just say what I think you said? Sure you're feeling okay?" She was slightly skeptical of his words, but after looking intently into his eyes, she believed the tenderness, the love she saw there. His strong, handsome face brought a sweet smile to hers. "And, I—"

"We've got to get going in a few minutes," one of the medics called out as he tended to Lester's needs and prepared him for the jostling ride through the forest on the stretcher. He was alert now and needed strong pain medication. Fortunately, the medics had plenty of that. Ivy wouldn't need to whip out any dried dandelion roots, although secretly, she wouldn't mind chewing on a few, hoping they'd dull her pain.

"Time to go. Even that small chopper is in big demand this week. The pilot won't want to wait too long."

Troy nodded and picked up the boy. Ivy began to pack up. "Leave it, darlin'. You've done enough. Rick and Stan said they'd clean up the site, put out the fire, pack up, and bring the horses home."

Lester moaned with each step the men took as they carried his stretcher over the rough terrain. Between his painful groans, he repeated the same five words over and over. "I don't deserve your help."

The first time he spoke, one of the medics replied, "Sure you do." After many repetitions of the phrase, the other medic, likely tired and stressed from the trek to the helicopter, said, "Well, you're getting it anyway."

The remainder of the walk to meet the helicopter was somber. Even little Billy must have picked up on the mood. He didn't say a word or crack a smile until he saw the larger-than-life helicopter parked in the clearing. "We get to ride in that?"

The medics matched Billy's enthusiasm. "Seems we'll be riding to the hospital in one of the best medevac choppers in the state. Oh, yeah, we'll be riding in well-equipped style."

THE FBI AGENT was there to greet them as they entered the Emergency Room. Lester on a gurney and Billy in a wheelchair. Troy and Ivy walked in without assistance.

Hospital personnel kept the agent at bay until all four patients had been examined. By the end of the day, Lester had undergone surgery on his leg, and Billy's arm was in a cast. The doctor said the boy was lucky. His primary injury was a clean fracture, and he'd be released that night.

Due to their similar medical needs, Troy and Ivy spent most of their hospital time together in a curtained–

off section of the Emergency Room. To pass the time, Ivy asked Mr. Storyteller to tell her a story.

"Hmm, let's see. Okay, I've got one."

*Once upon a time there was a rancher who needed some advice. Along came a man made of wisdom who helped out. Right away, that rancher sold off more than a thousand acres so he'd have the money to build a cabin, put up fencing, buy some cows, and rebuild the old barn that was the original building on the property. But something was missing.*

Troy told the story with passion, drama, and a faraway look in his eyes. Ivy enjoyed every word and wondered how his story would end. He continued.

*Leaning up against the crumbling old barn, his eyes closed, he tried to figure out why he felt so empty. A faint whinnying sound caught his attention. Or was that the wind? There it was again. He walked to the backside of the barn, following the soft sound. There it was. A sad-looking, brown horse with a black mane. It was so skinny the rancher could easily count its ribs. The horse needed him, and he needed the horse. That rancher and that horse have remained together to this day.*

"Whoa! That rancher was you, huh?" He nodded. "And the horse was Tracker. What an incredible story." Then it dawned on her. If that was a true story, Troy was the owner of The Lonely Horse Ranch. Suddenly, everything made sense. No one else claimed to own the ranch, and—

"It's your turn to tell me a story," Troy said, putting a halt to her new suspicion.

"I'm not a storyteller."

"That is an unacceptable answer. You are a story writer and—"

"Mr. McAllister?" asked a man standing at the edge of the curtain.

"That's me."

Ivy stared at the stranger. She'd been saved by the arrival of a man wearing hiking boots and jeans. Her story-telling duties postponed, at least for a while.

The man examined Troy's face, looking closely at the cuts and the bruising and pressing gently on his jawline.

"You're going to have some scarring there, my man. It's too late to prevent that, but it is something we can fix down the road. Just let me know." He handed Troy a card and left the room.

"That man is a doctor?"

Troy stared at the card in his hand. "Yes, a plastic surgeon."

Ivy bit her lip to keep from making a comment. She wanted to hear Troy's reaction first. He was a handsome man that took pride in his looks. How would he feel about scars on his face? No verbal reaction came, but he had a response. He tore up the card and tossed it into the trashcan.

Based on the results of Ivy's and Troy's X-rays and ultrasounds, they'd be released tonight, too, but were instructed to return if new pains or symptoms arose. Time would heal their wounds.

Saige rushed in with three sets of clean clothing. One for Troy, one for Ivy, and one for Billy. "I had to shop for the child's clothes." She turned, wrapped her arms around her boss, and broke down in tears. "I thought you died. I thought all of you were dead." She slumped down on the closest chair.

Ivy kneeled in front of the woman and held both of her hands. "We've all been through so much. It's going to take time to feel – I don't know – normal."

## TWENTY-SEVEN

Troy was glad to be back at the ranch, though the presence of investigators added to the tense, edgy mood brought on by the recent deaths. The extra vehicles, the yellow crime tape, and the smashed–up walls from the goons' clumsy attempts to find imaginary hidden treasure increased his anxiety. Unable to sit still or relax, he headed to the livery stable. He'd always been able to think more clearly in the company of horses.

Though far out in the pasture, Tracker galloped toward Troy like a racehorse, snorting, neighing, and tossing his head. He was the first to arrive at the gate between the large corral and the pasture, and was, without a doubt, on edge too.

Cody came out from the tack room and said, "Yeah,

your boy's upset. Rick said he didn't take well to trekking through rough terrain with a dead woman on his back. You want me to put him up in his stall?"

"No thanks, Cody. I've got this." Troy reached up and rubbed the broad, flat space between the horse's eyes and nose the way its mother would have done when he was a colt. His concern for the horse eased his own unrest.

"How'd it go at the hospital?"

Troy turned and saw his brother walking toward him. He hadn't realized until today they looked so much alike even though Trace was three years younger. "Okay, I guess. Lester needs more surgery and will remain there for about a week. The kid's arm is in a cast, a blue one. He thinks it's cool. I'm going to arrange for him to stay here for a few days. Ivy and I are banged up and sore as hell, but nothing serious. We'll be fine."

"You said that like you two are a couple. Are you?"

Troy hesitated, though not for long. "Yes." He had no doubt about that but wondered if Ivy would have given the same answer.

"Good. I'm happy for you. Oh, I did give mom and dad a call yesterday."

"How'd that go?"

"I didn't say much. When I told them I was here visiting you and your ranch, they were thrilled. I mentioned that some thieves were here causing trouble, and we were handling that. I didn't want Mom to worry any more than necessary, or Dad to show up. He does like to *fix* things."

"Well, I'm darn glad you showed up. If you hadn't, the body count would have been much higher. Thanks, Trace. How can I ever repay you?"

"Just be my brother, for real."

Neither spoke for a while. All Troy could do was nod and continue to rub Tracker. Being together after all these years was awkward. As boys, they each did their own thing with an ever-present undercurrent of hostility. Sibling rivalry? As adults, the resentment continued. Living in different states became a good excuse to leave things the way they were. Neither wanted to deal with it. Though neither knew what *it* really was.

Troy broke the silence. "Come on, I'd like to show you the far side of the ranch and the breeding barn. It's fun having the dude ranch, the guests, the horses, a few cows, but my main interest is in horse breeding and training."

They walked and talked. Tracker followed behind, no lead rope needed.

"I take it this bay is your personal favorite?" Troy nodded. "He looks a lot like my horse. They could almost be twins."

Troy almost smiled. "I guess there's one thing we

have in common: our taste in horses. Though I didn't find this horse. He found me."

He enjoyed telling his brother all about the stud horses and the breeding mares, but once they arrived at the facility, he showed off the amazing barn and spirited horses. Usually, only clients saw this side of his business.

"These two mares are pregnant. We should have two new foals in a few weeks."

He knew a sly smile spread across his face as he jingled a set of keys. Not seven, only three, but they were valuable keys. Keys that would never be part of any story.

"You asked if I had treasure. I suppose I do. Just never thought of it in those terms before. Not the kind of treasure Mr. V was looking for, although if he knew the value of what's behind door number two, he might have been."

Troy inserted one of his keys into what looked like one of many knots in the rustic, wooden wall. Turning that key made the wall move to the side.

"This is really wild stuff, Troy." Trace just shook his head.

Behind the wall stood several custom-made, stainless steel, state-of-the-art refrigerators filled with the world's best medications, supplements, and frozen horse semen.

Trace asked his first question. "Does dad know about all of this?"

"I don't know. We don't talk much. He never really liked me."

A look of shock flashed on Trace's face. "I always thought he liked you better than me, and then he proved it by giving you this amazing ranch property."

"I'm pretty sure he gave me the ranch to get rid of me."

In Troy's mind, there was sufficient proof of his dad's negative feelings toward him. As a kid, he'd cried over a cat. A McAllister man shouldn't act that way, and he'd often bragged about owning the Colorado ranch someday. Dad didn't like his arrogant attitude. "I wanted to run away when Dad told me I was too soft and you, Trace, were perfect."

"He said I was perfect? That's hard to believe. Dad was tough on me, too, Troy. I think he just wanted to make sure we grew up to be strong men. And it looks like we did, though we lost each other in the process."

Both men agreed they had a lot to talk about. A lot of catching up to do. "Why don't you join Ivy and me for dinner at my place? You're welcome to bunk there for as long as you want. I've got an extra bedroom." Troy may have spoken too soon. He hadn't been home yet. Would there be food in his kitchen? Would there be holes in his walls? What damage might the treasure-seeking goons have done? He grew anxious to wrap up the tour of his breeding facility and hurry home.

The two men walked and talked a bit more on the way to Troy's residence. Stopping outside the front entrance, Trace said, "That sounds like a good plan for tonight, but I'll be leaving early tomorrow. Got to get back to the Lucky 7."

"I'd completely forgotten about that small ranch. So it's still one of the McAllister ranches?"

"You *have* been out of touch. That's where Hannah lives. It's her ranch now." Trace's voice sounded so grounded, so loving. "She's the reason I'm here."

Troy shook his head in disbelief. *Who is this woman that's placed a spell on my brother?* He wanted to know, and he'd get some answers over dinner.

"Would you mind going to Ivy's cabin and escorting her back here? It's getting late, and I don't want her walking in the dark by herself." Trace headed out, happy to help any way he could.

Troy's residence had been spared destruction, likely because Lester had previously searched this structure or the goons ran into Ivy before reaching Troy's home. Therefore, the cooking commenced. He'd prepare a simple, but elegant meal to thank his little brother. He'd been a lifesaver. If he were able to impress him at the same time, so much the better.

Except for the moonlight streaming through the windows, the sky was completely dark by the time they sat around the dining room table. Troy held a bottle of wine in his hand and asked, "Any takers? This Pinot Noir will go well with the salmon teriyaki we're having tonight."

"Salmon? Not beef? I thought that was always a rancher's first choice." Trace seemed surprised.

"I had enough beef to last a lifetime before being banished to Montana." With the wine bottle in one hand, Troy set down a salad bowl with the other. "So, Pinot all around?"

Ivy agreed with his choice. Trace simply stated that champagne was the only alcohol he drank. Unfortunately, Troy was out of champagne. "Could you make due with Chardonnay or sparkling water with lemon?"

"The water sounds good to me."

"So, you only drink champagne?" His brother's limited use of alcohol brought a smile to his face. Or did he drink a lot of champagne? Or was that his way of being cool, sophisticated? No. Even as a teenager, Trace didn't need to be cool, but Troy? He was cool to a fault.

"That's right. Ever since dad's accident, the thought

of alcohol turns my stomach. I seem to be able to tolerate a glass of the bubbly now and then."

Ivy looked back and forth at the two men and their strange conversation like a spectator at a tennis match. "Accident? I feel like I've just walked into the middle of a movie without a clue."

"Interesting. You drink only champagne now and then, and I don't drink at all."

Ivy frowned. "Wait just a darn minute. You always matched me drink for drink. We drank red wine."

"My glass contained grape juice."

"What about beer? I've seen you drink a beer or two."

"My glass was always filled with tea."

The confusion on her face was adorable. When her hands went to her hips, he knew he'd be wise to change the subject, but Ivy had more to say.

"And what about the times you ordered your 'usual'? You said it was a Seven and Seven. I suppose that was water and water."

"Nope. It's half 7-Up and half diet 7-Up. Come on, let's eat."

Trace laughed between bites. The drinking conversation brought to mind an ancient memory. "You used to get into trouble whenever you told lies, and you did that often."

"You've got that all wrong, brother. As I recall, I often told stories, and I still do. Ivy can vouch for that."

"Dad didn't see it that way," Trace chuckled. Then Troy laughed and Ivy joined in. The remainder of the evening was priceless. A real family gathering. An experience Troy had long given up on.

"You'd said that Hannah was the reason you were here. Mind bringing us up to speed?"

"Hannah and I had a rocky beginning filled with vandalism, stalking, theft, attempted murder. You name it, we experienced it. We survived, but not without scars. The way she came through the danger and the trauma was remarkable. We fell in love and now we're engaged."

Troy tilted his head. "Hmm." And gave Ivy's hand a gentle squeeze.

"The moment I mentioned I had a brother that I hadn't seen in years, Hannah insisted that I fly right up here and visit you and your ranch. She's thrilled to be part of a family and have a future brother-in-law. She wouldn't take no for an answer. So, here I am."

Troy and Ivy exchanged glances, awestruck by the similarities in their stories and eager to meet Hannah as soon as possible. They agreed to share the details of their experiences one day when they were all together and the horror wasn't quite so raw.

That night, Trace slept in the guest room, Shadow

spent the night in Kitchi's cabin, and Billy stayed with Saige. Ivy and Troy lay wrapped in each other's arm wondering what tomorrow would bring.

Troy's conflicting thoughts disturbed his sleep for hours. *I'd kept my family members at a comfortable distance for so long. Now, it seems that phase of my life is about to end. Do I like that?*

## TWENTY-EIGHT

Ivy pretended to be asleep, while dozens of thoughts bounced around in her brain keeping her awake. They say money can't buy love, but it could buy informants and their knowledge. Even though the FBI said their first priority was to locate Lester's granddaughter, Troy also hired a detective to search for her and gave him an unlimited budget to bargain with. One way or another, the young girl would be found.

By the sound of Troy's breathing, she knew he was awake too. "I enjoyed meeting Trace, in spite of the circumstances. And his fiancée, Hannah, must be lovely and smart. I think we'll get along great." She hesitated to speak her next thought, a topic she hadn't wanted to bring up, but it was time.

Ivy learned more about life, death, and love in the

past two weeks than she'd ever thought possible. But now, she'd come face to face with the inevitable. Her flight back to Denver left the next day. Her great escape from the EMT job and her debut as a writer were winding down swiftly.

"I have a hunch it won't be long before we get together with Trace and Hannah."

Troy, propped up on one elbow, stroked her cheek and kissed her nose. "Why so sad tonight?"

"Is it that obvious?"

He nodded. "What can I do?"

Ivy puffed out a long sigh. "This is my last night. I'm scheduled to leave tomorrow. It's time for me to go home. We'd had so many other things to deal with, I let myself forget there was an end to my stay at the ranch and my time with you."

He pulled her closer and held her tighter. Physically, they were a good match, and she loved the scent and the feeling of his skin touching hers. Just like Trace and Hannah, they had a rough and rocky beginning. Maybe there was hope for them, and perhaps he'd invite her back someday.

Troy sat up and moved to the edge of the bed.

*Noooo! He wouldn't leave me alone again, would he? Not tonight of all nights.*

She watched unsure as he remained motionless and wondered if that was his silent signal for her to go.

He drew in a slow, deep breath followed by a record breaking, lengthy sigh. "Ivy… Please don't go." His words caught her off guard, but in a split second, she joined him on the edge of the bed. "Move in with me. I need you. The ranch, your pup, even Billy needs you. He told me he wants to live here, and I said that was fine with me. At least until he's safe and settled in with his uncle in Oregon."

She stood and then straddled his lap. "You're a good man, Troy. I do love you; I'm certain of that. And I don't want to leave, but I'm scared. Everything has happened so fast. Are we ready for such an arrangement." Tenderly, she held his face with her hands. "And, I don't want to take advantage of you."

*Should I stay or should I go?*

Although Ivy appreciated his invitation, additional thoughts complicated her decision. When she'd received the shattering, medical news about her inability to bear children, she immediately squashed any thoughts of motherhood or a family of her own. No man, especially a guy like Troy, would put up with such a deficiency.

But she couldn't ignore the fact that the pup and the boy reignited her motherly desires. Desires she'd attempted to extinguish before arriving at the ranch.

Could she live under the same roof with Troy? He had flaws, but so did she. She didn't want to get her hopes up for a fairytale life with a happily ever after. There was no such thing.

"Ivy, you would not be taking advantage of me. And, any time you want to leave, I will do my darnedest to change your mind, but if I fail, I'll help you get back to Denver."

She had to come clean before they went any further. It was now or never. Silently, she counted down from three and then blurted out, "Troy, I cannot bear children." Shaking, she held her breath trying to keep her heart cold and still waiting for him to pull away. Instead, he lifted up her face and looked lovingly into her eyes.

"I'm not so sure I have what it takes to be a dad."

Unsure of the meaning behind his words, it was good enough for now. "We're some couple, huh?"

Gathering her into his arms, he showered her with kisses, pausing only to say, "We sure are, darlin'. Together, we'll figure it out, one day at a time."

———

THE NEXT MORNING they found Shadow in the kitchen lapping up a bowl of Kitchi's newest batch of puppy food. She bounded over to Ivy as soon as her tummy was full and gave wet kisses to her favorite human the instant she was picked up.

Laughing, she held the tiny creature close. "I missed you, too, Shadow." She looked at Troy with raised, questioning eyebrows. Would he ask about "Shadow's mystery" or would she need to be the one? It didn't matter, as long as the question was asked. She glanced at Kitchi, then at Troy. Kitchi seemed oblivious to her signals, but Troy got it. He shrugged, then proceeded.

"Have you got time to explain what you meant when you said that the mystery of Shadow's untimely presence in the woods was solved?"

"I do. But I'll need to keep working while I talk, and due to my story's complexity, you'll only get the short version this morning."

They both shrugged and nodded in agreement. "That'll do for now," Ivy said.

"Do you remember Molly Enteman, Troy?"

"Sure do. She was our first and only neighbor. Haven't seen her in several years. That old lady sure loved animals."

"Yes, and they loved her. She'd feed any wild animal willing accept her gifts. Turns out she's got dementia and thinks she is Mary Ingalls."

His explanation was moving along too slowly for Ivy. "What does this woman have to do with Shadow?"

"She has no family to look after her, but keeps company with the wild animals."

"I think I saw her in the woods not long ago. I tried to help her, but she disappeared." Shock was written all over Troy's face. "I had no idea that was Molly. She said her name was Mary and she reminded me of a troubled homeless woman. She wanted nothing to do with me or the help I offered."

"Apparently, a pair of coyotes lived with her inside her house. Shadow was one of her wild animal friends' pups. When she took a few of those coyote pups for their first outing to the forest, the one in your arms got away."

Ivy held Shadow close to her heart realizing the miracle that had occurred. If she hadn't found her when she did, the pup would have died. But her thoughts quickly turned to the plight of Molly. Molly Enteman. "We've got to find her, help her."

"I made some calls while you were on your way to rescue Lester and the boy. She is in good hands for the time being, though I doubt she'll remain there for long."

Ivy's creative juices cascaded like a waterfall, and story ideas took over until Troy nudged her. "We should go to Saige's cabin and pick up Billy."

They thanked Kitchi for his good deeds knowing the topic of Molly Enteman, AKA Mary Ingalls, would come up again.

Billy was excited to see them. The foursome enjoyed the fresh air and exercise. Any onlookers would see a perfect little family: a mom, a dad, a child, and a puppy. For a while, Billy stayed between the two adults holding their hands, and Shadow followed behind. Before long, the boy let go. He and the pup ran in circles, jumped and played like two kids, or was that more like two puppies?

"Be careful, you don't want to damage that cast," Ivy called out. She looked up into Troy's sparkling eyes. "This feels good, huh?"

He admitted it did. "So you'll stay?"

She nodded and jumped into his arms, wrapping her legs around him. That was how Kitchi found them when he rode up on one of the quads. "There's a lady back at The Lodge that needs to see you, Troy."

"What does she want?"

"I do not know. She did not say, but her name tag spelled out: Cheryl Loftus, Social Services."

"Tell her I'm on my way."

Kitchi rode off, and Ivy's feet slid slowly to the ground. "Maybe she has news about Lester's grand-daughter."

"Maybe. I'd think that news would come from the investigator though. Come on, everybody, let's go say hi to Ms. Cheryl."

A woman stood on the front porch of The Lodge, her

eyes watching them approach. She exuded an aura of efficiency and an all-business appearance. She bent down and held out her hand. "You must be Billy. How are you today?"

"I'm great." He was all smiles and so adorable.

"Wonderful, I'm glad to hear that. I'm going to find a forever home for you."

Troy's expression darkened, and the empty, childless hole in Ivy's gut suddenly returned.

Billy's tiny voice broke the awkward silence. "I'm staying here with Mr. Troy, Shadow, and my mommy." He crossed his arms. For the moment, he was running the show.

"Billy, honey, we both know your mommy is gone."

"No," he shouted, now clinging to Ivy, his arms wrapped around her leg. "She's right here."

Ivy's eyes filled with tears. Troy spoke close to Cheryl's ear. "Wasn't Billy on his way to Oregon to live with an uncle?"

"He was. We've been in contact him, but he changed his mind." Her voice became a whisper. "Doesn't want him now, and we can't force the man to take him. "

Troy paced, but kept his eyes focused on Ivy and Billy now sitting on the steps with a coyote pup at their feet. He blurted out, "Well... we want him, and he wants us. So, make that happen."

The social service worker's face lit up. "I had no idea you were Mr. and Mrs. McAllister. I'd be delighted to begin the process to make that happen."

"Great. We're not married, so you'll want to use the name Ivy Radcliff on any paperwork you create."

"Oh." Cheryl's happy face deflated like a punctured air mattress. "Then I have to take him with me. That is the reason I was sent here today, I'm sorry."

Billy would not let go, so the woman pried the tenacious boy from Ivy's arms. He cried all the way to her car looking back over his shoulder.

The pitiful sound broke her heart and inflamed Troy. He stomped toward his office, then turned back. "I'm calling my lawyer."

Ivy trembled when the door shut with a bang. She sat, feeling sorry for Billy as well as herself, and held Shadow like a baby.

## TWENTY-NINE

Three days had passed. The investigators finally vacated the ranch. Troy made plans for repairing the devastation caused by the intruders while waiting impatiently for a call from his lawyer.

He was grateful Ivy had stayed and spent most of her time by his side. He kissed her often during daylight hours and held her sweet, naked body every night. She was the bright spot in his life twenty-four seven.

They didn't talk much about Billy, but Troy knew he was on Ivy's mind. For a brief time, her hopes and dreams to have a child had almost come to pass. A miracle had brought him into their lives, and a woman named Cheryl had taken him away. If only miracles could be bought, he'd have ordered one that very day.

Unfortunately, life didn't work that way. Not even for Troy.

Three bleak, but necessary tasks occupied their time over the next few days. In spite of rules and regulations, Troy had promised Jack's wife that he'd personally go back to retrieve what might be left of her husband. Officials had already bagged up Billy's escort's remains.

"Are you sure you want to go with me, Ivy? It won't be pleasant."

"I'm positive. This will be harder for you than me because Jack was your friend. I do want to accompany you if you don't mind."

"Don't mind at all. I'll ask Kitchi to pack a trail lunch and several sturdy laundry bags."

Ivy stuffed an additional set of clothing for each of them into a duffle bag in case the weather changed. "I'll meet you by the main corral."

Three horses stood at the hitching post, saddled and ready to go by the time Troy arrived. Cody had seen to that. "You didn't saddle Tracker?"

"No, boss. After seeing his reaction to carrying the dead woman from the crash site on his back, I thought you'd want to spare him from reliving that kind of trauma."

Troy nodded. "Good thinking. Thanks."

As soon as Ivy arrived, they mounted up and headed

north. The string of horses that made this journey twice already had left a visible trail to follow. They arrived in half the time. Troy was pleased to see that his wranglers had left almost no trace of their wilderness command center, which made being there somewhat easier.

Troy grabbed the bags, and Ivy took hold of his hand. With heavy steps and heavier hearts, they made their way to Jack's final destination. Neither had been near the plane since it burst into flames. The ground surrounding the area was covered in soot. The plane's shell was charred and its front end crushed, but it still resembled a small aircraft.

Troy handed one bag to Ivy and asked her to look around for any objects in the nearby area that someone might want to have. He took the other bag and cautiously entered the plane hoping to find something for Jack's wife to bury.

He found more than he expected. His stomach churned and his heart raced when his eyes focused on the mummy-like skeleton of his friend. He had to do this, but his own body would not cooperate. Instead, it became rigid, paralyzed.

"Everything okay in there?" Ivy called out.

He must have taken too long to answer, or uttered no answer at all. By the time the thick fog lodged in his brain cleared, he was standing outside with Ivy, a heavy bone-filled bag in her hand. She said softly, "Let's go. We can talk later."

They silently rode back to the ranch, each reflecting on the day's events. Cody took one look at them and said, "Go home. Rest. I'll handle the horses," he paused, "and everything else." They followed his suggestion without comment or question.

Once inside Troy's home, they stripped down and, side by side, slid into the hot, soothing water of the Jacuzzi. Troy lifted her hand to his lips and kissed it. "Thanks for your help today. You were amazing. I was—"

"Shh," she put a finger to his lips. "You were in shock seeing your friend in such a... a horrible state. Your reaction was perfectly normal."

He stroked her hair lovingly. His next kiss was right on her mouth. Deep, slow, sensual. He needed more. He wanted all of her. Though the rest of the evening lacked spoken words, Troy and Ivy communicated effectively with their bodies, each needing to escape the burden of their recent events and take refuge in each other.

---

IVY MET with Lucy and the minister from the church she and Jack belonged to. They planned a small memorial service that would take place on the ranch the following week. Jack's remains, mostly bones, would be buried in his family plot near Bozeman. Lucy's strength puzzled Ivy until the woman said, "If he had to die, it's good flying a plane occupied his final moments. He would have wanted it that way."

She dabbed away a single tear, and a sweet but distant smile appeared on her face. "He always made me feel like I was his first and only love, but I knew flying was a close second if not a tie."

Troy went back to the crash site with two investigators. Because the pilot was deceased and, therefore, no incident report filed, the FBI was involved. The NTSB had sent the small Go-Team to wrap up the aviation aspect of the investigation.

Even though a helicopter would fly them most of the way, Troy had said they'd hike that final mile in and out. The investigation could take most of the day, but Ivy didn't mind. She welcomed some alone time with Shadow. Her puppy had been with Kitchi a lot every day since her kidnapping. Starting today, that would change. She lived with Troy, and now, Shadow would too.

## THIRTY

Lester remained in the hospital for a week and inquired every day about his granddaughter's whereabouts. He never once asked about his daughter-in-law, the child's mother.

Ivy visited the man a couple of times, and though Troy never left the ranch, he and Lester spoke on the phone daily.

"I've been thinking about a few things," said Troy.

"That makes two of us, Mr. McAllister. I don't know why you even talk to me, but I'm glad you do." Only silence flowed across the airwaves. "I'll be out of your way as soon as they release me. That FBI lady has likely picked out a place for me to stay… for a long time."

"I don't know much about that. Come live at the ranch for a while after you're released from the hospital.

That'll give you time to fully recuperate while you await news of your granddaughter."

"You're very kind, and I would like that. Do you think I'll be allowed to leave the hospital and head to your ranch?"

"You haven't been officially arrested yet. And I over-heard some talk about the possibility of immunity for you."

Troy knew that scenario was in the works as long as Lester testified against Mr. V and Mutt. *Hmm. Mutt.* It didn't matter what the guy's real name was, he'd always be Mutt to Troy and Ivy.

Troy's attorney had been able to arrange for Billy to visit the ranch every other day until a suitable foster family took him in or he was adopted. Ironically, Billy's escort's body was shipped to Chicago where her only living relative resided.

A Chicago PD officer found little Ella, Lester's granddaughter, sitting on a bench in Jackson Park. After a thorough medical exam, detailed questioning, and several psychological evaluations, the child's missing-in-action mother sent her to stay with Lester at the ranch. Her reason? She wanted Ella to be far away from the area where she'd been held captive. At least that is what she said before taking off on another trip.

Troy moved Lester and Ella to a two-bedroom cabin.

She was delighted to be with her grandpa, the horses, and Billy on his visiting days. They were best friends from the moment they met.

Troy cooked most of their evening meals at home, but when Billy visited, the boy always wanted to eat in the dining hall. He'd insist they invite Lester and Ella. Every time, he'd spread his arms wide and say, "It's just like havin' a great big family." He was so cute and happy in spite of the recent trauma he'd gone through and what appeared to be a sad past. Troy's attorney promised more details about the child would be forthcoming.

"Ivy, got any plans for this evening?" Troy had a plan. A master plan.

"Let me think. I've already worked out. I've made good progress today on the outline for my story. We're not expecting any guests. Nope, no plans for tonight other than loving you and Shadow."

"Great. Meet me in the spa promptly at seven o'clock. I have an errand to run right now, but I shall return." He turned and walked out the front door. He didn't look back but felt certain her face held a confused look of suspicion, and her hands were on her hips. Oh, yeah, he had a plan.

Ivy was right on time. He found her wrapped in a large blue towel, her hair gathered on top of her head, and sitting on one of the spa's padded chairs. "I wasn't sure if you wanted me here or actually in the water at seven. You weren't specific enough."

Though difficult, Troy kept his tone serious. "No need to quibble over semantics, but yes, ma'am, I want you in the water." His clothes were in a pile on the floor before she'd slipped the towel from her shoulders. They entered the soothing, hot water together.

"So, this is your plan?" Her nose wrinkled and she squinted.

"Part of it. Thought we'd begin our evening by soaking the day's stress away. We'll only be here for a few minutes."

When a few minutes had passed, he got out of the water and motioned for her to stay. He returned with two thick, warm robes better than any 5-star hotel offered. He covered his naked body with the largest of the two and held up the other one for Ivy to slip into.

"This is a nice surprise. Thank you. I guess you went shopping today." She stood on tiptoes and planted a kiss on his lips.

"I thought we should be warm on our walk to the loft."

"The loft? You know me and heights. I'll never make it up that steep ladder wearing this huge robe."

"It will be warm in there, so you'll be able to take

your robe off. *I'm counting on the robe being off.* You won't fall. I'll be right behind you."

"Okay." She shrugged, her face showing skepticism.

Troy gave her a smile and a bear hug, and they began the walk in the cold night air. He knew she had unpleasant memories from their last time in the loft, but tonight's plan would override them all.

Outside the double doors, he took out a blindfold. "Would you mind if I put this on you? Just for a minute?"

Ivy shook her head and squeaked, "No."

Once inside, he removed the blindfold and studied her reaction. Her jaw dropped, and her eyes widened. "Oh, Troy. You did all this for me?"

Indeed, he had. The steep ladder had been replaced with an actual staircase that included a railing. The side of the barn where the plane had been parked was walled off with potted pine trees. The temperature warm, the lights dramatically dimmed, the aroma of something delicious wafting through the air were all part of his plan. He could tell she loved it.

He bowed at the bottom of the stairs. "After you, m'lady." To his delight, she removed her robe before heading upward. *God, she's gorgeous.* He picked up the robe knowing she'd want it later.

A plate of assorted gourmet finger food including cheeses and red grapes sat in the middle of the small table. A bottle of grape juice on one side, a bottle of wine on the other. He pulled out a chair for her to sit on, then began to pour wine into her glass.

She stopped him. "No, I'll have what you're having. I insist."

Troy poured the juice and slipped her robe over her shoulders.

They toasted their love with grape juice and had eaten only a few bites of food when Ivy discarded her robe for the second time. Letting her hair down, she whispered, "Let's make love. Right now."

She needn't ask twice. Troy led her to the bed, but rather than lay down he sat and patted the space next to him where she was to sit. Could he go through with the rest of his plan? Never in his entire life did he think he'd be doing what he was about to do. Never!

He choked on his words, but when he opened the velvet jewelry box and she saw the diamond ring sparkling in the candlelight, she threw her arms around him. "Yes! Yes! I'd love to marry you." Tears of joy spilled from her eyes. "But what about—"

His lips on hers delayed the remainder of her comment. He slipped the ring on her finger. "We'll start figuring everything out tomorrow. Tonight is for expressing our love."

## THIRTY-ONE

"Good morning, Cheryl, Troy McAllister here. Ivy and I have some news to share. A wedding is in the works." They held hands, full of anticipation.

"Congratulations. I assume your wedding plans include a ring and a date?"

Only fifty percent of her assumption could be answered with a resounding yes. Ivy's head nodded up and down urging Troy to speak the affirmative answer out loud anyway.

"Yes, Cheryl. A ring and a date."

"In that case, I'll create the necessary documents to make this ranch Billy's temporary residence with the two of you as foster parents, for now. Let me know when that

wedding takes place and we'll begin adoption proceed-
ings. If that's what you want."

That was exactly what they both wanted.

"I know Billy has visited you at the ranch several
times and he always returns happier than before. With
that said, how soon do you want him to arrive and stay?"

Troy looked at Ivy; Ivy looked at Troy. "Today!"

———

THE BETTER PART of the afternoon was spent placing
online orders of furniture and decorations that would turn
the guest room into a little boy's room within the week.
They'd almost completed that task when Billy arrived.

"Can I pick out the cover for my bed?"

Troy whispered in Ivy's ear, "Does he mean a
bedspread?"

Ivy nodded. "Or a comforter."

"You sure can. Let's find a good one." Troy set Billy
on his lap. Come to find out, the boy was quite the shop-
per. Finding the 'good one' took until dinnertime. The
one their little buckaroo eventually chose looked nothing
like a child's comforter, but more like a wrangler's bed
cover decorated with pictures of horses. Real horses.
Billy gave Ivy a huge smile and threw his arms around
Troy's neck.

"I'm the luckiest kid in the world. I've got two super-heroes of my very own."

---

AFTER TUCKING BILLY INTO BED, Troy and Ivy agreed to inform their families about the engagement before the word got out around the ranch. Ivy chose to call her brother tomorrow morning. They rarely spoke and a call from her this late in the evening might startle him. Troy, on the other hand, wanted to startle his parents and couldn't wait to give them the news. They'd been pestering him about settling down for over a decade.

"Ready?" Ivy asked.

"You bet I am." All smiles, Troy pressed the phone number for Clint and Alice on his cell phone. "Dad? You're about to be a grandpa."

Ivy's jaw dropped, then she whispered, "No hello, no small talk first"?

He grinned and shook his head.

"Now, Troy, listen to me, son. You know I'm over-joyed, but you need to give some thought to the order of things."

That was so typical of his dad. He always had to be in charge, put in his two cents. But nothing was going to rain on Troy's joyful, fun-loving parade tonight.

Ivy whispered, "Shouldn't we explain the situation a little?"

Troy smiled. "Not yet."

Clint had more to say. "Don't say another word until I get your mother on the line." They could hear him call out, "Alice, dear. It's Troy. It seems he has something to tell us."

"Troy, dear, what a surprise. It's so good to hear from you. So, you have some news? I hope it's good news. Tell us everything."

"Mom, you're going to be a grandma. But our story is a long one and needs to be told by two storytellers... in person. How soon can you get here?"

End of Book 2

In The McAllister Brothers Series

**Author's Note**

I knew long before the release of Colorado Takedown that I'd write a sequel. Why? Out of the blue, another cowboy entered my thoughts, demanding attention. I named him Troy. He would be Trace McAllister's older brother. Book 2, **Montana Countdown,** is his story. By the time I began to develop the premise, the main events, the characters, and the conflicts, I'd experienced another year's worth of outdoor mountain adventure, and a whole lot of knowledge about family dynamics—especially where brothers were concerned.

I used this knowledge to create the issues and the tension between Troy and Trace. I'd known women who instigated tension between brothers as well as those who softened such hostility. For this book, I chose the softer side of problem-solving… and moved forward with what would someday become a ranch family saga.

Readers often ask me, "Where do you get your ideas?" The truthful answer is, "From everywhere, from everyone, and everything." I know, I know. That is a very unsatisfactory answer. Ideas bombard me every minute of every day. There's no stopping them. So, I keep a hand-held recorder nearby – unless I forget it – to avoid losing a gem of an idea. Aha! That is what Ivy, this novel's female protagonist does too. See what I mean?

One day, as I skimmed through this novel searching for a passage to read aloud at a book event, I noticed an abundance of similarities to my life right there on those pages. Things I hadn't thought of in years, not even during the writing process. For example, Troy was a storyteller, a guitar player, and a singer. Me too. He demanded symmetry and neatness. Yeah, I've been accused of that. Ivy kept a medical secret and would rescue just about anything – even bugs. Little things for sure. Nevertheless, I hadn't consciously included them in the story. Still, there they were. Both Ivy and I have a fondness for coyotes and story writing. Hmm.

I hope you enjoyed Troy's story. Now head on over and give Book 3 a try. There, a father's challenge puts his sons in danger, but their women have a better idea. If it works, they'll celebrate Christmas together. Read about family, fate, and a life-threatening contest in WYOMING SUNDOWN.

**Cricket**

*What's Next?*

## WYOMING SUNDOWN

Book 3 in The McAllister Brothers Series

Trace and Troy agree to take their dad's challenge and ride horseback across the remote wastelands of Wyoming with Christmas just weeks away. Three men in danger, three women worry. What could possibly go wrong?

**What? You missed Books 1?**
**No problem. It's never too late.**

## COLORADO TAKEDOWN

Book 1 in The McAllister Brothers Series

A vegetarian from the city and a cattle-raising rancher sounds like a match made in hell. But what if they need each other more than they realize?

## THANK YOU!

Thank you for reading *Montana Countdown*.

Would you like to know when the next book in the *McAllister Brothers* series is available? That's easy. Sign up for Cricket's (almost) monthly NEWSLETTER and you'll receive notifications of new books, giveaways, and other exclusive content.

If you enjoyed this story, please leave a REVIEW on Goodreads, Bookbub, or your favorite online retailer. Reviews are helpful to readers and appreciated by authors.

# ABOUT THE AUTHOR

Cricket Rohman grew up in Estes Park, Colorado and spent her formative years among deer, coyotes, and fields of beautiful blue columbine. After retiring from a career in education, she became a full-time author writing contemporary fiction and western series and sagas about teachers, cowboys, dogs, lovers, and creative women inventing unique careers—just to mention a few.

Cricket loves to hear from readers.
Connect with her via:


Website http://www.cricketrohman.org
Facebook https://facebook.com/CricketRohmanAuthor
Twitter https://twitter.com/CricketRohman
Bookbub https://www.bookbub.com/authors/cricket-
rohman
Email cricketrohman@gmail.com

## MORE BOOKS BY CRICKET ROHMAN

You will find the links & excerpts for all of Cricket Rohman's books at

**www.cricketrohman.org**

**The McAllister Brothers Series**

*Romantic Western Adventures*

COLORADO TAKEDOWN, Book 1

This twisty cowboy adventure includes treachery, new love, family, courage, and amazing ranch animals.

MONTANA COUNTDOWN, Book 2

A wealthy rancher's story-telling tendency entices two eavesdroppers—a greedy criminal and a would-be novelist—to venture to his Montana ranch to search for his hidden treasure.

WYOMING SUNDOWN, Book 3

Clint McAllister's challenge put his sons in grave danger. Alice is furious about his foolish plan. It was almost Christmas, a bad time for such nonsense.

**The Creative Hearts Sweet Romance Series**

*Creative Women Standalone Novellas*

## PHOEBE'S PHOTO FETISH

Phoebe Foxglove had three loves: Photography, Flowers, and Bobby. Two out of the three served her well.

## ANNA'S ANIMAL HOUSE

Anna's new life began the moment she caught a glimpse of the flashing red light. There was no turning back now. But what was up ahead?

## CAITLIN'S COW WASH

Caitlin feels trapped and out of place living in an old-fashion *Leave It To Beaver* household. Then, a perfect, win-win solution comes along—a cowboy named Cooper.

## TINA'S TASTY TOURS

Tina has an impossible dream that comes with a substantial price tag. In the meantime, she works at the Punk Patio and a 1960s diner where she is required to look like Marilyn Monroe.

**The Lindsey Lark Series**

*Fiction with Elements of Romance & Mystery*

### WANTED: AN HONEST MAN

Lindsey, a kinder teacher in survival mode after an unthinkable divorce, is brilliant in the classroom. Unfortunately, unwanted sinister challenges invade her off-hours.

### LETTERS, LOVERS, & LIES

Jake and Lindsey are in love, but so much stands in their way. Fortunately, they are smart, multi-talented, and they love to laugh. Wendell, the 180-pound mastiff, is featured throughout this series.

### HIT THE ROAD, JAKE!

Thrilling, romantic, and sprinkled with humor, this novel reinvents the 'buddy movie' concept with the written word … and a pretty woman. As Jake and Lindsey travel from Tucson to Estes Park in their RV, the dangers they face become deadly.

**The Fantasy Maker Series**

*Contemporary Adventures*

### FOREVER ISLAND

JD won a contest and ended up on a deserted island somewhere in Micronesia. This is a wild beach adventure complete with danger, love, and a dog named Noodles.

### WINTER'S BLUSH

The Fantasy Maker strikes an agreement with Clay. What's the catch? He must pretend to be someone he's not. A quick read that includes mountain hiking, rescue dogs, danger, and yes, some romance.

## Saving Madeline

*Standalone Contemporary Fiction*

An entertaining story with humor, emotion, and an unusual mother-daughter relationship.

## Christmas in the North Woods

*A Children's Picture Book*

Oliver Owl introduces the reader to his forest friends who are busy rehearsing for the annual Christmas Song Contest.

www.ingramcontent.com/pod-product-compliance
Lightning Source LLC
Chambersburg PA
CBHW061129200626
46817CB00016B/465